**GRACE FOX ANDERSON** is publications editor of *Counselor*, Scripture Press' take-home paper for children 8 to 11. She has been in church-related work with children for more than 25 years. Mrs. Anderson received her degree in Christian education from Wheaton College, Wheaton, Ill. Her stories and articles have been published in a variety of Christian magazines. She has also compiled the other stories in the popular Winner Books' Animal Tails series: *The Peanut Butter Hamster and Other Animal Tails, Skunk for Rent and Other Animal Tails, The Incompetent Cat and Other Animal Tails,* and *The Duck Who Had Goosebumps and Other Animal Tails.*

# SKUNK
## FOR RENT
### (and other Animal Tails)

*edited by*
## Grace Fox Anderson

*illustrated by*
## Darwin Dunham

**A WINNER BOOK**

**VICTOR BOOKS**™
A DIVISION OF SCRIPTURE PRESS PUBLICATIONS INC.
USA CANADA ENGLAND

CREDITS: "A Skunk for Rent," "Old Red," "Miss Miranda's Babies," "Porky, the Impatient Porcupine," and "Nuisance in Ma's Kitchen" all were previously published in *Discovery* by Light and Life Press, Winona Lake, IN 46590. "Unusual Escort" and "The Champ" were previously published in *Teen Power,* and "Stubby and the Christmas Miracle" was previously published in *Connect,* both products of Scripture Press Publications, Inc. "Dogs Are Your Friends," "Skippy and the Cat," "Punkin and Princess Make Peace," "Creature Features," "Animal Fun," "God's Special Gifts," "All for a Duck," "My Dog Valley," "Floss Finds a Friend," and "Buttons" were all previously published in *Counselor* by Scripture Press Publications, Inc. "Little Forest Friends" was previously published by The Salvation Army in *The Young Soldier.* "A Home for Everyone" and "Perfume Sprayer" were both previously published by The Mennonite Publishing House in *Story Friends.*

*Fifth printing, 1987*

Most of the Scripture quotations in this book are from the *King James Version.* Scripture quotations marked (NIV) are from the *Holy Bible, New International Version,* © 1973, 1978, 1984, International Bible Society. Used by permission of Zondervan Bible Publishers.

Library of Congress Catalog Card Number: 81-84126
ISBN: 0-88207-493-8

VICTOR BOOKS
A division of SP Publications, Inc.
Wheaton, Ill. 60187

# Contents

# A Skunk for Rent

## A FICTION STORY by Betty Steele Everett

NICK looked around eagerly as he opened the door to Mr. Born's pet store. Right away he saw two black-and-white skunks in cages. And one of them was his! All Nick had to do now was give Mr. Born the money he had been saving for almost a year. Then he could take the skunk home for his very own pet!

"Hi, Nick. Come to get your skunk?" Mr. Born asked.

Nick nodded. "Yep! I've got the money right here in my pocket. I'm going to call him 'Stripe' because of the white stripe down his back. Are you sure he can't spray anymore?"

Mr. Born laughed. "If he could, he would have by now. The men who raise skunks for pet shops take care of that when the skunks are babies. But the skunk doesn't know he can't spray. If he gets frightened, he'll still try."

Nick was counting out his money when the pet shop door opened and a woman about his mother's age came in.

"Oh, you have a skunk! Thank goodness! I've been so many places—" She opened her purse as she came toward Mr. Born. "How much is it? Will you take a credit card?"

"It's $50," the pet store owner said, "but I'm afraid neither of these is for sale. They've already been sold. Nick's here to pick his up, and the other one's spoken for too."

For a minute the woman looked as though she might cry. Nick was glad when she smiled instead. "Nick, I'm Mrs. Wilson," she told him. "My little girl, Melanie, is about your age, and she's very sick. She's allergic to cats and doesn't like dogs. She wants a pet very much—something she can play with. She read about skunks as pets and wants one. I've been trying to find one for her, but they're hard to come by."

"But Stripe's mine!" Nick said. "I've been saving for him for a long time. Skunks only come once a year."

Mr. Born nodded. "I can only get them once a year and never as many as I could sell. That's why they're always sold before they get here. If you want to put your name down for one next year, I can save you one then."

Mrs. Wilson shook her head. "Melanie needs one now." She turned to Nick. "If I paid you $55 would you sell your skunk to me? You'd have enough to buy one next year and $5 more."

Nick shook his head. He had told all his friends about coming to get Stripe. They would all be waiting at his house to see his skunk. He wanted to have Stripe to show them. He didn't want to wait another year to get his pet.

"Please!" Mrs. Wilson said. "I'll make it $60!"

Nick looked over at Mr. Born for help, and the pet store owner stepped between him and Mrs. Wilson.

"I'm afraid it's not for sale, ma'am," Mr. Born said firmly. "How about a hamster or a gerbil?"

"No, I'll keep looking," Mrs. Wilson said. "I'll call the pet stores in the city. Surely one of them will have a skunk."

Nick took Stripe on the leash Mr. Born had given him. He felt proud as he walked along the sidewalk toward home. Everyone he passed looked at him, then turned to look again. Nick laughed. No one could believe he was seeing a live skunk on a leash!

When Nick got home, the gang was waiting. "Wow! It really is a skunk!" Joe said. "Can we pet it?"

"Sure," Nick said. "It plays like a kitten. In fact, Mr. Born told me a baby skunk is called a kitten."

"I bet you're the only person in this whole town that has a skunk for a pet!" Joe said. "Neat!"

"Someone's buying the other one Mr. Born has," Nick said. "But he doesn't live in town." He suddenly remembered Mrs. Wilson. "I guess there will be another one soon, though. Some lady was in the store trying to buy one. She said she'd go to the city and look. She wanted to buy Stripe, but I wouldn't sell him. She wants it for her little girl—she's sick."

Joe looked at him quickly. "I bet it's Melanie Wilson! She's really sick."

Nick was surprised. "You know her? I never heard of her before."

"They just moved in down the street a couple days ago," Joe said. "They're only renting that house, though. Mom went over to call on them, and Mrs. Wilson told her how sick Melanie was and that they didn't want to look for a house to buy till Melanie was better and could go with them. I've never seen her, though, I think she has to stay in bed a lot."

"Maybe her dad could go out to the woods somewhere and catch a baby skunk for her," one of the other boys said.

Nick shook his head. "No! Mr. Born says that's really dangerous. Any skunk you want for a pet should come from a pet shop. Melanie'll probably have one soon, but if she's sick, how will she take care of it?"

Nick and his friends played with Stripe the rest of the afternoon, and no one talked about Melanie again. But Nick kept wondering if her mother had found a skunk for her.

That night after dinner Nick took Stripe for a walk. Then, when he had put the skunk into its box for the night, he went to his room to get ready for bed. As he took out his Bible to read the passages for that day listed in the Sunday School lesson for Sunday, Nick thought about Mrs. Wilson again.

"Please help her find a skunk for Melanie, Lord," he prayed. "Joe says she's really sick and has to be in bed a lot. Please help her get better too."

Nick turned to his Bible and the lesson, but he could not keep his mind on what he was reading. Finally he sighed. "Mrs. Wilson must have found a skunk for Melanie! And Stripe is mine! I paid for him and I told her I wouldn't sell him! But if Melanie's sick—"

Nick went to the telephone and dialed information. The woman gave him a number for a Wilson family living on Joe's street. Nick wrote down the number, then just looked at it for a long time.

"Please, Jesus," Nick prayed, "please let Mrs. Wilson have found a skunk for Melanie."

His heart was pounding as he dialed the number. It rang three times and Nick felt a rush of hope. If no one answered, it wouldn't be his fault. He would have tried. But he knew he would have to let it ring longer to be fair.

Then a woman's voice said, "Hello?"

Nick's mouth was dry and he swallowed. "Mrs. Wilson? This is Nick—the boy at Born's Pet Shop. The one with the skunk. I was wondering—well, if you'd found a skunk?" Nick held his breath, praying she would say she had found one for Melanie at another pet store.

"No, Nick, I didn't." Mrs. Wilson sounded tired. "I called all the pet stores in the city, but none of them have any skunks that aren't already promised. I told Melanie I'd try some other places tomorrow."

Nick held the telephone tightly. He did not want to sell Stripe. He had already told Mrs. Wilson that. Then he suddenly remembered what Joe had said about the Wilsons renting their home now. They lived in the house, but they did not really own it.

"Mrs. Wilson," Nick said, "would you like to rent Stripe? I mean, I could bring him over to your house on my way to school and leave him for Melanie to play with all day. Then I could bring him home in the evening. She wouldn't have to take care of him much, and she could play with him. You could buy some food for him sometimes."

"Rent a skunk?" Mrs. Wilson was suddenly laughing— or crying, Nick wasn't sure which. "Oh, Nick, we'd love to do that! Melanie was so disappointed when I couldn't find one for her. But now she'll have one to play with whenever she feels like it. When can you bring Stripe?"

"Tomorrow morning. Tell Melanie I'll be there and so will Stripe."

He hung up and went back to his room. He felt a lot better now. Stripe would still be his, but Melanie would have a pet too.

# Perfume Sprayer

by Gloria A. Truitt

I dine on mice and insects . . .
   Ripe fruits and berries, too . . .
And if deodorized I'll make
   A friendly pet for you!
My spray does not cause blindness . . .
   As some believe . . . that's bunk!
By now I'm sure you've guessed that I'm
   That creature called a skunk!

# Sandy Takes a Shortcut

A FICTION STORY by Cynthia Hettinger

"GINNY!" Sandy called as she ran through the snow to the barn, her long auburn braids flying. "Where are you?"

No answer.

A week ago the girls made plans to meet today at 1 o'clock sharp and ride their horses together.

Peanut, Ginny's sorrel mare, stood quietly in her stall. The barn was deserted. *I'll get Carbon ready. Ginny will be here by then*, Sandy thought. She was anxious to get out.

Carbon's warm breath splashed against her cold face as she slipped into her horse's stall. She pulled off his heavy winter blanket and stepped back to admire the black gelding. He was her 11th birthday present. She'd owned him over a year now.

Happily, she brushed his warm hair, then remembered that she had promised her mother she would never ride alone on the trails.

"I wish Ginny would hurry. Guess I'd better phone her," she said, slapping her horse on the side. A dusty telephone sat on the old table in the tack room. "Ugh, no answer," she grumbled after trying to get her friend.

She looked up at the wall clock as she picked up her saddle. "It's 1:45 already. If Ginny isn't here by the time I'm ready, I'm going alone."

The snow squeaked underfoot as Sandy led Carbon into the sunlight. After checking the girth, she yanked the stirrup down. "Stand still!" she commanded. The dancing horse calmed down as she stepped lightly into the saddle.

The tall gelding responded eagerly to Sandy's leg pressure. Across the road they picked up the trail around the pony farm's hillside pasture.

Straining his ears forward, Carbon moved out in a smooth trot. The pasture beside them seemed empty. Then came the quick sound of many ponies running: Da-da-dum! Da-da-dum! Suddenly they broke over the hilltop and galloped straight for Sandy and Carbon.

Carbon knew they were coming before she did. With a leap, he pranced toward the ponies.

"Whoa, fella! Whoa!" Sandy cried. But he bucked as the herd crashed against the fence separating them.

A tightly held fistful of mane was all that kept Sandy from falling. Finally, she managed to turn Carbon away from the other animals and back onto the trail. Then she let go of his mane.

"Wow! I'm glad that's over!" she exclaimed.

Once in the woods with its twisting path leading over snow-covered logs and under half-fallen trees, they slowed to a walk. Sandy loved these moments and felt close to her horse.

In the open again, a long striding gallop sent two orchards and a hay field flying past. Slowing to let Carbon catch his breath, Sandy saw the sun hanging low in the sky. Time to head home.

As they returned through the orchards, Sandy noticed

a large flat field ahead. The pony barn's bright roof stood out above the trees beyond the field. "A perfect shortcut," she said, eyes sparkling.

But as they started into the field, Carbon stopped. Sandy jabbed her heels into his sides, but the horse planted his feet firmly.

Sandy spoke sharply: "Get moving!" Carbon wouldn't obey. She'd make him. She was determined to take the shortcut. Turning uphill, she broke a short branch from a tree.

Again they approached the field. Carbon stopped. The whip stung and he moved forward. Walking cat-like, he went about 30 feet when CR—ACK! CRACK! Ice cold water splashed over Sandy's legs as Carbon slid down into a frozen swamp.

Long fingers of icy water seeped down her boots and circled her toes. Sandy's mouth went dry. Her heart pounded. Suddenly Carbon turned and lunged toward shore and Sandy fell onto the broken, snow-covered ice.

It held! Looking up, she saw her horse gallop toward the woods.

"He doesn't seem injured," she said to herself as she crawled off the ice to solid ground.

Relief flowed through her when she stood up. She stared at the "field." Yes, it was a swamp with bushes poking through the ice.

Carbon had sensed the danger. Why hadn't she? "How did I ever get into this mess?" she asked as she turned and followed Carbon's hoofprints through the snow. She was shivering and couldn't stop.

Tears filled her eyes and slid down her cheeks. Was Carbon bleeding? Sandy knew her parents would punish her. She could hear Mom now: "Sandy, your responsibility as a child of God is to hear and obey. Love enables us to listen and do what we should. Remember, because of Jesus' great love, He obeyed the Father and died on a cross for our sins. The least we can do is obey simple rules at home."

*I do love my horse*, Sandy thought. *If only I wasn't so stubborn!* Beneath the wet jeans, her legs stung. She paused and rubbed them. "I'm sorry, Lord Jesus," she prayed, "please let Carbon be OK."

A horse and rider came trotting along the pasture as Sandy approached. It was Peanuts with Ginny and they had Carbon in tow.

"Sandy, what happened?" Ginny yelled as she rode up on Peanuts.

"Am I glad to see you!" Sandy said. She took the reins and bent her stiff jeans and mounted. Her toes smarted as she pressed her feet into the stirrups. Sandy described her disaster as they rode.

"Wow! Am I glad it wasn't me," Ginny said.

"Why were you so late?" Sandy asked as they neared the barn.

Ginny made a face. "I couldn't help it. I had some errands to run."

Once in the barn, Ginny commanded, "You check Carbon while I call your mom."

Sandy examined his legs. *No cuts, thank God!* Then she dried him off with an old towel and buckled on his blanket. Wrapping her arms around his neck she cried softly. "I'm sorry, Carbon. I promise I'll never lose my temper again. Please forgive me."

He lowered his head and nuzzled her as if he understood, and Sandy kissed his ear. As she closed his stall door, she breathed a prayer of thanks that the accident wasn't worse. "And please give me strength not to be stubborn and to listen and obey when I should," she concluded.

The girls sat on the doorstep to wait for Sandy's mother.

"Your mom's angry," Ginny reported.

"I probably won't be able to ride for weeks," Sandy said.

"You know, horses sometimes have quiet ways of speaking to us. I think it's a little the same with God," Ginny shared thoughtfully. "My dad says that God speaks in a still, small voice inside us after we ask Jesus Christ to live in us."

Nodding, Sandy added thoughtfully, "They both want us to hear and mind. Maybe from now on it won't be so hard."

# Stubby
## and the Christmas Miracle

**A TRUE STORY by Rickey Diamond**

AS DOGS go, Captain Stubby was a rather silly one. We only added "Captain" because he seemed so completely unaware of how funny he looked.

He was a mixture of cocker, Pekingese, and poodle—a cockapeekapoo. A short-legged dog, he had so much long blond hair that his only visible features were a black button nose on one end and a bouncing pom-pom tail on the other.

Mother had fallen in love with him. But Dad, who admired German shepherds with names like "Baron" or

19

"Caesar," never stopped growling about Stubby. "That isn't a dog!" he'd sputter. "That's—that's—absolutely useless!"

It was true. Captain Stubby only had two strong points: He would dance in circles on his hind legs for a special treat. And girls went wild over him. Otherwise, he bounced about tirelessly and barked at anything he imagined to be dangerous.

That first Christmas he spent with us, Captain Stubby wore an oversized red bow strung with bells that jangled with his playful bounds. It may have been that tuneful sound that made our Christmas seem unusually cheerful. "Thank You, Lord," I remember praying. "This is going to be a good Christmas after all."

Since I'd received the Lord Jesus as my Saviour, I dreaded all religious holidays. No one else in the family loved Him. They couldn't see why, for instance, I wanted to read the Christmas story aloud from the Bible.

But this year was going to be different. I could feel it.

Suddenly I heard Dad shout from the bedroom, "Stubby, give me that!"

Dad burst into the living room, chasing and finally catching Stubby and throwing him on his back.

"What are you doing?" Mother demanded.

"That fool dog has swallowed a needle!" Dad answered. He poked inside Stubby's tiny mouth for a trace of it.

The rest of us circled around to see for ourselves. Stubby, grateful the examination was over, panted happily. "Are you sure?" Mom asked. "Oh, he couldn't have! He *seems* all right."

"Of course I'm sure!" Dad cried. "I noticed the needle on the carpet because it was threaded. But before I could pick it up, Stubby ran off with it. Now he's swallowed it. He's a dead dog for sure."

Though we couldn't imagine how a little dog like Stubby could swallow a needle, Dad sounded sure.

Frantically, Mother and I called all the local vets. Of course no one was working on Christmas Eve. We figured that by the time they were back in their offices, the needle would have worked itself into some vital part of Stubby's tiny body.

There was nothing to do but bustle about, trying to cheer each other up again. We couldn't help looking over our shoulders at Stubby, however. Each time he made an unexpected move that might be the start of his death throes, we'd jump. This certainly wasn't the Christmas I had thanked the Lord for.

But gradually (I don't know how) an inner assurance gripped me. *It couldn't be God's will for Stubby to die today.* And then I heard God's voice, so clearly I remember jumping a little. "Go pray for the dog," He said.

Now there have been times in my life when I've longed to hear God's voice—times that would have seemed more fitting. But now?

I struggled for a moment with doubts, and waited for them to be answered by some brilliant argument from God. *Should I really pray for our dog? In front of my family? I don't pray in front of them about normal stuff. They'll think I'm crazy!*

Somehow the Lord's silence was a firmer command than an answer would have been. Scared as I was of looking foolish, I was more afraid of not doing what God had so plainly told me to do.

I crouched down beside Stubby, nearly doubling over so as not to attract attention. "Dear God," I began, trying to act natural.

"What?" I heard my mother call as if I had addressed *her*. "Whatever are you up to, Rickey?" she asked, as she

walked across the room to see what I was doing.

"I'm—er—praying for Stubby," I said, my face growing hot.

She stared at me—her son—in shock. But she didn't stop me. I went on, painfully aware that everyone in the room knew I was praying out loud, on my knees, for our dog.

It meant death to my pride to obey God in that moment. But the rest of me died by inches in the next few hours. *You must have been crazy to think you heard God speak. It was just your imagination talking to you. How are you going to explain things when he falls over dead?*

I kept a worried eye on Stubby, praying all the while.

When he bounced and danced, my hopes did the same. But when he coughed or sputtered, so did my faith. And when he lay down for a nap . . .

"He'll probably never wake up and just go in his sleep," my father said with certainty.

But Stubby *did* wake up, lively as ever. And gradually our frightened glances in his direction grew fewer and everyone joined in what proved to be a jolly Christmas after all.

I actually felt confident by the time we all went to bed. I even reminded Mom and Dad of my prayer and that God cares about everything that matters to us.

Several days went by with unsinkable Stubby feeling no ill effects. Secretly, I began to suspect that he had never swallowed the needle. Dad was sure though, and the whole family seemed certain *something* slightly miraculous had happened. I liked the way our family talks were going, so I kept my doubts to myself.

Three weeks after Christmas, Dad called to me. He sounded excited. "I've got to tell you what happened. You know that useless dog?"

*Uh-oh. That needle finally caught up with him. Now how could I explain things?*

"Well, I don't know how it happened, but he just coughed up that needle, neat as you please! It's a nice long one too. And it's still threaded!"

"What?" I said, hidden doubt betraying me. "How could he?"

"I don't know," Dad said, laughing. "By rights it should have stuck in his throat on the way up. But he's still bouncing around like he owns the place."

I was amazed to hear my father say, "You know, son, I think God waited just to prove He really *did* work a miracle."

My parents are both Christians now. So you see, the story of Captain Stubby isn't just another dog story after all. God used our silly little bundle of fur to teach us all something about Himself—for one thing that "the foolishness of God is wiser that man's wisdom" (1 Cor. 1:25, NIV).

# Old Red

## A TRUE STORY by Marie M. Booth

MAMA WORRIED a lot about the chickens. They roosted on the front porch. They dropped piles of smells. They made dusty holes between the weeds, where they lobbed around, frittering up clouds of dust. Papa said that was the way they cleaned their feathers and skin, but Mama sent Marie out to shoo them back to the chicken house. They never stayed.

When it rained, they gathered under the back porch or bunched against the sides of the log walls. They really wanted the front porch but Mama shouted "No!" and they moved off in a huff.

Not impressed by the name-calling, they gathered themselves up pencil-sharp, tails drooping, and stood in the drip, eyeing her accusingly.

One big red rooster, head tall to Marie's waist, quarreled about the injustice. He ruffled himself—he grumbled. He tramped his big, yellow feet up and down across the porch. His feet were fully eight inches from spur to toe and were attached to legs as scaly as tree trunks.

After every showdown with a human being whose back was turned, he would gather himself up into a rage. He'd

25

split like lightning, ski on spikes and wing, scattering rocks and dirt, bringing himself up sharply in a furious cloud of dust right at the heels of his tormentor.

At this point, his glistening red feathers would settle innocently back to shape. He would lift his red comb to its full height and stand tall, challenging anyone to name him anything but a fine fellow.

But his eyes would turn as red as his disposition when he saw Marie coming. Lowering his head, shaking the floppy red comb over one eye, he would slim himself for the attack and roar off at her fleeing back, grabbing black stockings, dress, apron strings, flying arms!

Having chased her through the back door, he would lift his great feet, preening and strutting. A hen passing by would get a severe peck on the head for not recognizing his majesty.

For weeks, Marie and old Red glared at each other. Marie never let him get at her back. She gathered the eggs at dusk after Red had taken charge of the roosting pens, settled several quarrels, created a few of his own, and was about ready to mount the poles.

By this time of day, there was no one to watch his victories, so he red-eyed her as she stealthily searched out the eggs and went on fixing his feathers for the night.

One day Red was meaner than usual. Torn and bitten, Marie was tired of the big bully. She was determined to get the eggs while it was still daylight. She got herself a big stick, and carrying her basket over one arm, she slipped out of the house. To fool old Red, she walked all around the house, keeping out of sight. Coming out on the other side, and now sure she had outmaneuvered Red, she ran for the chicken house.

But he was waiting. He aimed his head and took a piece of black stocking from the fleeing figure. Marie whirled

and swung at the rooster with the stick. He sidestepped and appeared to withdraw. With extravagant indifference he pecked on the ground.

Ah-ha! She had him bested—but she'd keep that stick! Marie gathered the eggs—a basketful—and cautiously poked her head out of the chicken house, planning how she would make it safely to the house.

Red was generously sharing his bits of grit with a circle of hens when he saw Marie coming. He paid her no mind. She circled wide, keeping him to her front and keeping the stick poised. Suddenly he burst into a rage! With wing-span of some four feet, and spurs like hooks, he flew to the edge of her basket, sending eggs scattering.

Too scared to use the stick, Marie turned to run. Not satisified with the damage done, and whipped into a frenzy of triumph, Red flogged her back with his wings all the way to the house. Marie stumbled through the door, came to rest on her bottom, sliding crazily in broken eggs.

Disgust was giving way to rage, but not to pain. She was too mad to suffer! Mama bathed her scratches and pecks and kissed her red face, but she could do very little for the welts across her shoulders. Comfort flooded Marie only temporarily. Every time her wounds wakened her in the night she gritted her teeth and planned to get even.

The next morning Marie sat on the kitchen stoop, a long keen switch across her knees. Her pants rinsed of egg, hung on the clothesline. They flew as a battle flag this morning. She sat with her back against the door. Every time Red came near she entertained herself with thoughts of a half-dozen grim things that would happen to the old buzzard. That's what he was—a buzzard! Papa said those birds sailing around in circles were hovering over a dead carcass—or one they thought would be dead in a little while. "Well, Ole Red, I'm not about to be dead!" she muttered.

The rooster ignored her. Even though the hens found the corn first, he stepped through the circle of biddies and found one fat yellow grain. He picked it up, flicked it down, and generously called his ladies to come get it. They pretended they had not seen the kernel and ran obediently—usually ending up in a slight scuffle.

Red straightened to his full height and craned his neck to eye Marie. He must get closer—but he couldn't get behind her. Pecking and calling, Red led his flock right up to the stoop to study the situation.

Marie bounded off the step and brought the switch down on his head and back. Once on the run, she switched him all around the house. Back to her post, she mounted her step and waited. Taken by surprise, the rooster withdrew and adjusted his misplaced feathers.

This was not the way the game was supposed to go! He'd lure her off the step! He gathered his flock and

pecked and scratched, disappearing behind the chicken house. It didn't work. Marie never left her stronghold.

One thing for sure, Mama would send Marie to shoo them back if they ganged up on the front porch. So, after an hour of innocent maneuvering, Red wound up on the front porch with his flock. Sure enough he heard, "Marie, go run the chickens off the porch."

Red chuckled. He'd pretend to be roosting. Suddenly Marie burst through the front door—long switch coming straight at the rooster. Unable to gather himself for attack, he fled. Red zigzagged across the yard trying to throw her off, but she beat the air, his back, his head—all around the smokehouse, all around the chicken house!

The feud went on for days. Marie never came out without her switch. And she used it every time the rooster came in sight. She gathered the eggs whenever she chose. If he came in sight, she set the basket down and chased him out of sight.

Losing face, old Red lost interest in the game, and Marie came and went as she pleased. Sometimes, if his eyes got red and he came too close, Marie jumped at him with both feet. At first he scattered, but at last Marie allowed him his dignity when he calmly sidestepped her bluster. That began a long and uneasy truce on both sides while Red grew old and Marie grew up.

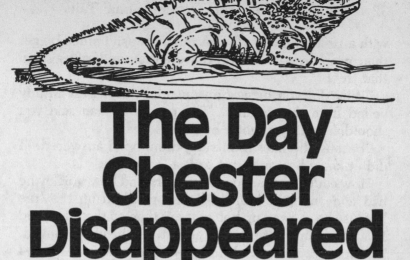

# The Day Chester Disappeared

A TRUE STORY told by David Hope
Written by Barbara L. Hope

"OH, DAVE, be careful!" Mom shouted from the ground. "Don't fall!"

I was at the top of our apple tree in Marion, Ohio, bending down to try to find Chester, my new iguana. (An iguana is a kind of lizard.) Right then, I don't think I cared if I did fall; I was so mad at myself for losing Chester.

I thought maybe I could find him if I looked down from above. His coloring was a perfect camouflage. He was light yellow-green on the bottom and a darker leaf-green on the top. His tail had narrow brown rings, just like a twig. He even had a ridge of spines on his back that matched the edge of an apple leaf.

Chester was just a baby iguana—a hatchling, the pet store owner had called him. I had just bought Chester the day before. He cost $20. I had earned the money collecting old newspapers for recycling.

Right away I had measured him. His body was 4″ long

with a 10″ tail. Except for his tail, he wasn't much bigger than an apple leaf. And there were thousands of leaves in that tree!

"Why did you bring him outside?" my sister Mindy yelled from the ground. "The pet store man said you shouldn't until you got a harness."

"Because he likes it outside, dummy!" I answered. "I didn't know he could run so fast."

How could I get anyone to understand how quickly he had gone up that branch? I had put him on the tree because he showed up better there than on the grass, and I watched him every minute at first. But he never moved. I turned away to watch Mindy—for just a second. When I looked back, Chester had climbed up the branch.

I reached for him, and he lifted his body up on his legs and hopped. It was as if he were playing tag with me. He always hopped just a little farther than I could reach.

I finally had to climb the tree. When I looked down to find a place to put my foot, he had disappeared. I couldn't see him anymore—anywhere.

I whispered, "Dear heavenly Father, please help me find Chester. I know I shouldn't have brought him out here, but I didn't think he was going to get lost. Please help me find him! In Jesus' name, amen." I had received Jesus as my Saviour when I was seven, and I knew I needed His help.

I hopped down from the tree and went in to get Mom. She ran out and looked up at all those leaves on the tree for a minute. "Oh, honey, it will take a miracle to find him now," she said.

She closed her eyes to pray, and I got a ladder for her from the garage. Then I climbed the tree again.

My friend Rodney came over to spend the night. He climbed the ladder while Mindy looked all over the grass.

I kept moving from one branch to another, but I just couldn't see anything.

Then our neighbors, Mr. and Mrs. May, came out to help. "Maybe we should try to think like an iguana," Mom said. She laughed, but I didn't think it was funny.

Mr. May just stood by our porch and stared at the tree for about 10 minutes. Finally I thought, *Boy, he's not much help.*

Just then he said, "I see him—at the end of that branch." I couldn't believe it!

I started down out of the tree in a hurry, but Mr. May said, "Easy now, don't scare him." So I got down as quietly as I could and tiptoed to where Mr. May was pointing. Sure enough, there was Chester at the very tip end of a little branch.

Mr. May never took his eyes off Chester. He told me to move the ladder over so I could reach Chester. I did, and climbed up the ladder as slowly as I could: reached out with both hands to catch the iguana if he moved, putting one hand on the branch behind Chester and wrapping the other around his body.

Poor Chester, he was shaking badly, and I had to pry his claws off the branch. Then he dug into my T-shirt and held on tight. I kept my hand over him all the time, though, so he couldn't hop away.

We all thanked Mr. May and found out that he really had thought "like an iguana." He decided Chester would be so scared, he'd probably go as far away from the noise in the tree as he could. The farthest he could go would be the end of a branch. Mr. May had looked slowly at the tips of all the branches in the part of the tree where I said Chester had gone until he finally saw him.

Rodney and I talked a lot about what had happened to Chester. He said, "I was so worried, even *I* prayed."

He came over a lot after that to see Chester and went to church with me a couple of times. I don't think Rodney's a Christian yet, but he listens to the teacher.

I made a little harness out of an old boot for Chester to use outside, but he doesn't like it much, so I usually keep him in the house. He likes to climb on curtains and swim in the bathtub. He always finds a new place to hide when I let him out of the cage.

Even Mom says Chester's no trouble now, but once in a while I think about the day I almost lost him. If God would help us find a little green lizard, I guess He'll take good care of us too.

# Miss Miranda's Babies

## A FICTION STORY by Sharon B. Miller

JANELLE SAT on the back porch and watched as Miss Miranda waddled across the backyard, followed by her four tiny babies. *Baby ducks have to be the cutest things there are*, Janelle thought with a sigh. She rested her chin in her palm, her elbows on her knees.

*Well, sitting here isn't going to solve my problem*, she thought. She got up and went into the house. Her mother kept cracked corn in a large bag for Miss Miranda. Janelle filled a cup and took the corn back outside.

She was careful to feed the ducks away from the back porch. Her mother didn't like the ducks to be up around the back door.

"Here, Miss Miranda," Janelle called.

The mother duck hesitated just a moment to check her babies trailing her. Then she waddled quickly over to Janelle.

It was so much fun to watch the tiny ducklings grab a piece of the corn in their small bills. They would lift their heads high in the air, shaking them to wiggle the corn down. Then they'd grab another piece as if they were sure there wouldn't be any corn tomorrow.

Janelle set the cup of corn on the ground, and when Miss Miranda wasn't looking, she grabbed up one of the ducklings. Quickly she covered the fuzzy little duck with her hands and stroked it to calm it.

Miss Miranda could get pretty upset if her babies started calling for help. Janelle's little brother Stevie had been chased and nipped on the leg by Miss Miranda only last night.

Finally the corn was all gone. Miss Miranda called to her babies and started to the pan of water by the garage. Janelle put the baby duck down and picked up the empty cup. She went back to the porch and sat on the top step.

*It sure would be nice to be a baby duck*, she thought. *They don't have any worries at all. Someone feeds them and waters them every day. They have Miss Miranda to protect them.*

"Hi, Janelle, what's the matter?"

Janelle looked up as Loni, her best friend, rode her bike up to the back porch and got off.

"I've got a problem," Janelle admitted.

"Can I help?" Loni asked.

"Sure." Janelle grinned. "Can you give me $3?"

Loni shook her head. "You know I never have any money."

"Well, I guess you can't help," Janelle said. "I need $3."

"Sorry," Loni said. "Maybe you'd like to ride down to the store with me. I have to get some milk for my mother."

"I'd better not," Janelle said. "My mom will probably want me to help with dinner soon."

"See you tomorrow, then," Loni said. She turned her bike around and started down the driveway.

Janelle sighed again and stared at the top step. A tiny ant crawled rapidly across the paint. It had seemed like such a neat idea to make a missionary pledge during the church service a week ago when Mr. George had visited their church and preached. He had told how many people were receiving Jesus as Saviour in the small village of Sinatu where the mission station was located.

Even though so many people were becoming Christians, there were still many more who had never heard of Jesus, Mr. George explained. These people lived in the jungles and villages, some in places that could only be reached by going down the river in boats. But it took money to buy the gas for the boats, he had explained; and the missionaries needed clothing and food as well as a place to live.

Janelle took a deep breath and let it out slowly. Miss Miranda had led her family back to the center of the yard. There they could find plenty of bugs to eat.

At the time Mr. George had presented the need, it seemed as if it would be easy to raise some money to help the missionaries. When the pastor had asked people to give money to help Mr. George go back to Sinatu with the Gospel, Janelle had known she wanted to help. When the offering basket was passed, she took one of the white cards. Out of the corner of her eye, she saw that her father had taken a pledge card too.

She had wondered just how much to give. Then she thought of $3. Even though she wanted to help, she had known that $3 was a lot of money for her to earn. If she couldn't find a way to earn it, she would have to save her allowance for 12 weeks. That meant no candy bars or ice cream cones. But she did want to give the money.

She had filled out the card and handed it to her mother. Her mom and dad both looked at it. They had smiled and nodded OK. So Janelle had placed the card in the offering plate. She had felt so good then. Her money would go to help take the Gospel to other people.

She shifted on the wooden step. Helping a missionary had seemed so exciting then. And she still felt it was pretty exciting. But where would she get the money?

Suddenly she realized Miss Miranda was at the bottom of the steps. The black-and-white mother duck was making small noises in her throat, begging for more corn. Her babies were busily picking in the grass around her.

Janelle stared at Miss Miranda and her babies. Then she had an idea. Quickly she jumped up and raced in the house, letting the screen door slam behind her.

"Mom! Mom!" she called.

"I'm in the the dining room," her mother answered.

"Mom," Janelle said as she dashed into the room where her mother was dusting, "I have an idea how to get the money for my missionary pledge." She stopped for a breath. "You know, Dad said I can only keep one of the baby ducks besides Miss Miranda. So my idea is to put an ad in the newspaper with our phone number, and maybe someone will buy them. That would give me some money to help pay my missionary pledge."

"I think you have a good idea," Janelle's mother agreed. "But why don't you call Mr. Harrison? He told your father that he would like to have ducks on his farm again. They have a pond, you know."

"I'll call him right away," Janelle said eagerly.

When she hung up the phone, she told her mother excitedly, "Mr. Harrison said he would buy all of Miss Miranda's babies I have for sale at a dollar apiece. I guess that's a pretty high price for baby ducks, but Mr. Harrison said they were so pretty he'd like to have them."

"You can deliver them right now, before dinner, if you'd like," her mother suggested.

"OK, Mom," Janelle agreed. "I'll put them in a box and take my bike. That is, if Miss Miranda is agreeable enough to let me catch three of her babies." She grinned.

"I'll give you a hand and distract her so you can catch them," her mother offered.

"Thanks, Mom," Janelle said. She turned to go outside, then she hesitated.

"I made a pledge, but I sure didn't know where the money would come from," she said slowly. "God supplies our needs just like He does those of the missionaries, doesn't He? Dad said I couldn't keep all of Miss Miranda's babies, and I sure hated to give them up." She smiled. "But, selling them to help pay my pledge isn't nearly as hard as just having to get rid of them. And, I still do have one baby duck, plus Miss Miranda."

Her mother smiled.

"Mom, I guess this proves that what Mr. George said is true. If you trust God to supply your need, He will take care of it—whatever that need is."

# A Home for Everyone

by Gloria A. Truitt

Pigs are happiest when they
   Can roll in mud and muck,
But lakes and rivers, streams and ponds
   Are best for Quacky Duck!
Bears prefer to make their homes
   In caves or hollow trees,
And birds snug in their nests of twigs
   Chirp morning melodies.

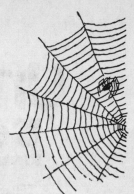

Each house is very special for
   They're built with care and love,
Including hives and spiderwebs
   And dovecotes for the dove.
But there's a house that I like best . . .
   It's made of wood and stone.
Do you know why I like it best?
   Of course, it is my *own*!

# Unusual Escort

## A TRUE STORY by Hal Olsen

SARAH ESAI looked out across Kenya, Africa's Great Rift Valley with concern. She bit her lower lip as she tried to decide if she should spend the night with her friends in the Kinari Forest or try to walk home before dark.

"You'd better stay here with us, Sarah," her friend Rachel Kamau said. "You've got your baby with you. It's not safe in the valley at night."

Sarah shifted the backrack holding her baby girl, Miriamu. She looked thoughtfully across the 35-mile wide valley.

"Thank you, Rachel, and you too, Yona," Sarah said, turning to her friend's husband. "But I really should try to make it home this evening."

She looked up. "From the angle of the sun, I'd say I have just enough time to make the 9 miles home before dark. Solotai would worry if I did not return home by nightfall."

Sarah was a new Christian. Her friend Rachel had taught her about Jesus. One day Rachel had urged Sarah to receive Jesus Christ as her Saviour, and Sarah had gladly done so.

Her life changed a lot after that. She no longer feared the evil spirits. Instead, she trusted the Lord. She prayed that her husband Solotai would also receive Jesus as his Saviour.

When Rachel Kamau moved to her husband's village way up in the mountain forest, Sarah missed her. She longed for a Christian friend since she was the only believer now in her village. That's why she had visited Rachel and Yona. Even though they were Kikuyu and she was Masai, Sarah loved to talk about Jesus and study the Bible with them, for Yona was a Christian too.

As she started toward home that evening, she walked quickly. Solotai was probably wondering when she would come home and cook his supper of cornmeal porridge. She pulled her deep red robe around her as she made her way down the mountain slope to the Rift Valley.

"Help me now, Lord," Sarah prayed as she entered the valley. "Help me to arrive home safely. Keep wild animals and bandits away."

Just then a herd of loping giraffes moved off into an acacia tree grove. The valley was loaded with animals: zebras, gazelles, eland, wildebeests, and warthogs. Then there were the dreaded hyenas, leopards, and lions.

For centuries her people, the Masai, have refused to eat any meat but beef. That means the animals in their part of Africa are plentiful because they haven't been killed for food. Only the white man hunts there.

However, sometimes Masai warriors hunt lions to prove their manhood. Sarah hoped that there weren't many lions in the area. Actually, she feared men more than animals. Most animals—even the more dangerous ones—would move away when a person walked near them. But she had heard of robbers attacking people who walked alone.

"I am with you always." She comforted herself with Jesus' words. Her baby whimpered and she began to hum the first Christian song she had ever learned: "Jesus loves me, this I know."

Mile after mile she walked. The sun was setting near the distant ridge. Sunset colors bathed the valley in an unreal gold. In the distance, she could hear the hammering of an anvil bird. She breathed in the sweet smell of cassia flowers. She felt good because she was nearly halfway home.

Suddenly, she stopped in her tracks. Ahead was a band of 20 or more baboons. She had never liked apes, but she had never really feared them. The village dogs usually chased them off. But now she was all alone! What could she do? She didn't even have a *simi*, a handmade knife carried by most of her people. "Father, help me," she prayed, open-eyed.

The leader of the pack made a move toward her; then the whole group did. But suddenly all the baboons screamed and ran off across the fields.

Sarah sighed with relief. But she couldn't imagine what had made the apes act that way. She thanked God for His deliverance, and walked faster. The sun was just slipping below the distant hills. She knew she had little time left before dark.

A sudden feeling that something or someone was following her made her stop and look behind. But she saw nothing and walked on.

Ten minutes later, she came over a slight rise and found herself walking headlong into a pack of hyenas, one of Africa's most hated animals. They were eating the remains of a zebra that had been killed by a lion. They cackled at Sarah in a bloodcurdling chorus.

All at once, unlike the fleeing baboons, the horrible

hyenas came straight toward her. Sarah closed her eyes in terror, waiting to be attacked by their razor sharp teeth. But the attack never came.

Suddenly, there was a deep-throated roar from the bushes behind her, and the spotted hyenas veered off and raced away.

Sarah turned quickly and saw her unlikely rescuer. A hundred yards away stood a black-maned lion. Looking both regal and deadly, the big beast stood his ground. He made no move toward her. Still looking fearfully over her shoulder at the lion, Sarah started walking on.

Finally, she took her eyes off the big cat and hurried toward her village. She went a quarter mile more before daring to look again. When she did, she was gripped with fear. The lion was still behind her. It had kept about 100 yards between them.

But Sarah forced herself to walk. If she ran, the lion might attack. On she went, praying all the while for God's protection.

Soon she came over the last rise before her village. In the fading light, she could make out the humped gray outline of the houses belonging to her people.

Just then she heard an animal take off into the grass. She wondered if this were a leopard or some other dangerous beast. And was it also escaping from the nearby lion? Again she looked over her shoulder. Yes, her follower was still there. Somehow she felt no fear now and walked the last half mile to her village with confidence.

As she entered the village, she took one final look at the lion. Then Sarah knew that God had sent him to protect her and her baby as they walked home. The lion stood silent, taking one last look at her. Then he trotted off across the plains.

"*Sopa*, Sarah!" the villagers greeted her. "It is good you have made it home safely!"

She purposely did not tell them about the lion. She did not want a band of warriors to run out and spear the animal God had sent to protect her.

She did, however, tell Solotai, her husband, about her escort. "We shall kill a goat and leave it outside the village as a sacrifice to the lion," he suggested.

"No, my husband," she said. "The lion was only a tool. It was God who helped me. He wants us to give Him nothing but praise, and I have already thanked Him."

# Little Forest Friends

by Gloria A. Truitt

Wouldn't it be fun to chat
  With little forest folk,
To sing with Mrs. Bobolink
  And answer Froggy's croak?
Wouldn't it be fun to play
  With Miss Petunia Skunk,
Or scamper with the squirrels
  Up and down a buckeye trunk?
If I could get just close enough
  To whisper in an ear,
I'd say, "Please let me play with you . . .
  Don't run away in fear!"

# Dogs
## Are Your
## Friends

By Bernard Palmer

ONCE a Minneapolis gas station operator was held up and robbed. It happened just after his German shepherd dog got back from obedience school. He had supposedly been trained as a watchdog. But he slept through the robbery, and when the police came, tried to bite them. Now dogs don't usually behave like that. Normally, a dog knows a friend from an enemy.

Most dogs are like Nero. Nero was a little cattle dog on a Midwestern farm. He made himself a hero by saving 10-year-old Grace, his owner, from an angry bull.

Grace was out in the pasture alone when the bull charged her. Nero heard her screams of terror and dashed out. Without thinking of himself at all, he leaped at the angered bull just as the animal was about to catch Grace on his horns. Nero chased the bull away so the girl could run to safety.

Of all the animal friends we have, dogs are some of the most useful and reliable. During World War II, officers discovered that a sentry on duty was far safer with a dog than with another man. Today, police dogs are invaluable

48

in fighting crime in areas where police*men* are not respected.

In the Arctic, sled dogs were the chief form of winter transportation for many years. Thousands of blind men and women use well-trained seeing eye dogs to take them anywhere a sighted person can go. Dogs have been trained to pull carts, track criminals, sniff out narcotics and hidden bombs. They can do many other tasks and do them well.

For many hundreds of years they have been kept by men for their company and help. The mastiff, greyhound, and Afghan hound are a few of the breeds still known today that lived even before Jesus Christ walked the earth. If you could put a mastiff puppy born in Jesus' time and one born today beside each other, you would not be able to tell the difference. The mastiff hasn't changed at all.

Dogs can be divided into three general groups: sporting dogs, working dogs, pets. Many breeds that are just pets today, of course, were developed for sport or work.

The collie, sheep dog, German shepherd, and Great Dane, are some dogs bred and trained to work. They looked after cattle or sheep, and guarded children or royalty.

Dogs developed for sport, mainly hunting, would be those such as the spaniels, setters, pointers, and hounds. Those chiefly kept as pets were chows, the Boston terrier, and toy dogs such as Pomeranians, and Chihuahuas (che-WA-was).

Most breeds were developed to serve a special purpose. For instance, the monks at the Hospice of St. Bernard in the 18th century bred Saint Bernards for rescue work high in the Swiss Alps. The English pointer was bred in England in the 17th century to find and point out game birds in brush and tall grass. Even the popular poodle was first bred for hunting.

When my grandfather moved to northern Minnesota a friend gave him a beautiful collie. He was a big-boned two-year-old named Jack.

My grandfather's farm wasn't fenced in then. Often the cattle wandered out into the woods and got lost.

One hot August afternoon, Granddad went out to look for the cows. For three hours he tramped through brush and swamp. Finally he turned back without finding a single one. At the door to the house, he stopped and looked down at the dog. "Jack," he said, half joking. "Go get the cows!"

To Granddad's amazement, the dog went trotting off into the woods. In 20 minutes Granddad heard cowbells clanging. Jack was bringing them in. Granddad hadn't known until then that Jack was a well-trained cattle dog. He was able to find the cows in a few minutes. But he was so well trained that he wouldn't go for them until his master told him to.

It takes awhile to train a good dog. You should start training him when he is about six months old and work with him at least half an hour every day. When you teach him, be gentle and kind, but firm. Your pup must learn to obey you.

If you want to teach him to sit, place your hand on his hindquarters. As you press down, say, "Sit." When he does so, reward him with a little piece of meat or something he especially likes to eat. And don't forget to pat him and praise him.

Don't try to teach your dog more than one trick or command at a time. When you give him an order, use simple words and as few as possible. People who have made a study of dogs say a dog can understand only 56 words at the most, though some dogs act as if they can understand far more than that. They remember words by hearing you use them over and over in connection with the thing you are trying to teach them.

If you start teaching your dog something like coming when called, don't stop working with him until he learns that particular thing. If you give up, he will get the idea that he doesn't have to obey. Then you won't be able to train him to do anything.

Use a rolled up newspaper if you must punish him. It makes a noise when you hit him, but it won't hurt him.

If you have a puppy at home, you should plan to train him. You'll enjoy doing it. Afterwards, he'll be worth a lot more to you as an obedient, clever pet.

# Skippy
## and the Cat

A TRUE STORY by Delores Elaine Bius

ROGER BIUS liked animals of all kinds. He was especially fond of birds and often envied their ability to fly. He had owned a couple of pet birds and now had a parakeet.

So it was natural for him when he found a baby robin in his yard in Chicago to make a pet of it. The bird had fallen from its nest and was too young to fly. Roger made it a cage out of a box, covered with screen wire. He named the robin Skippy.

For several days, Roger had to feed the robin every few hours. He gave it bread dipped in milk, earthworms, and hamburger.

52

Skippy grew fast. His breast got redder and his tail feathers longer. He was soon ready for his solo flight.

Roger took him outside and carefully threw him up in the air, only a few feet off the ground so he wouldn't be hurt if he fell. Skippy learned fast and soon knew enough to spread his wings and glide.

Each day Roger took him out in the backyard and placed him on a low branch. Skippy would perch there for hours, listening to the other birds and catching insects in the air. Soon he began to fly alone and soared higher and higher. However, he'd get scared and couldn't always come down from a high perch.

The first time he perched atop Roger's house, Roger had to get the ladder and bring him down. Later, Roger rescued Skippy from the roof of the garage, then from a low tree branch.

One day Skippy flew to the top branches of the tall cottonwood tree in the side yard. There he sat for hours, in spite of Roger's calling over and over. Eventually, Skippy flew down and perched on Roger's shoulder.

Skippy always spent the nights in Roger's room, snug in his box-cage. In the morning, he'd wake Roger up with his chirping. Roger would call, "Come here, Skippy." The robin would fly over and sit on his chest as if to say, "Wake up, you sleepyhead."

Roger's father urged him to let Skippy go. "He's going to be so tame that he won't be able to feed and care for himself," he told Roger. But Roger didn't want to let him go.

Then it came time for the family to go on their vacation. They were going to drive to Texas to visit grandparents. There was no way they could take Skippy. A friend would take care of the parakeet, but it was too much to ask her to care for Skippy too.

Roger decided to set Skippy free in the yard of his friend, Ben. Ben lived across the street and also liked birds. He promised to look after Skippy. Before the Biuses left, Roger took Skippy over to Ben's house each day till Skippy got used to Ben and would come when he called.

On the way home from Texas, Roger could hardly wait to see Skippy. When they reached home, he jumped from the car and ran to Ben's house. But Ben had bad news.

Skippy had stayed close to the house. He had especially liked to perch in a Chinese elm in Ben's yard. And he dug for worms beside a lilac bush in the fenced yard. Normally, it was a safe place for a robin.

One day, while Ben was weeding the garden, Skippy was hopping around, digging for worms. Suddenly, Ben spotted a furry creature out of the corner of his eye. He whirled around, but was too late.

Somehow the neighbor's Persian cat, Kit-cat, had gotten into the yard. He pounced on poor Skippy and made off with him in a flash.

Ben was so upset. All he could do was chase Kit-cat yelling, but it was no use.

Well, you can imagine how Roger felt. Never before had he hated an animal. But he sure hated Kit-cat. He felt worse because poor Skippy hadn't known that a cat spelled D-A-N-G-E-R!

Roger was determined to lie in wait and do Kit-cat in. In fact, he spent hours in the next few days, thinking of ways to get even with the cat.

When his parents found out why he was so moody, they began to talk to Roger. "The Bible says, 'Vengeance is mine; I will repay,' saith the Lord" [1] his mother quoted. "It's wrong for you to want to kill someone's pet cat just because it killed your bird."

"Yes, son," Dad agreed. "After all, it's the cat's nature to eat birds. You really can't blame the cat."

Roger thought the situation over for a long time, but he just couldn't get over his bitterness.

One day his mother said, "Roger, it's a sin for you to want to kill Kit-cat. Just as Skippy couldn't recognize the danger when he saw a cat, so you aren't recognizing the danger Kit-cat is to you.

"I'm afraid Satan is using Kit-cat to get at you. He's a roaring lion, trying to devour us, just as Kit-cat devoured Skippy. 1 Peter 5:8 (NIV) says, "Be self-controlled and alert. Your enemy the devil prowls around like a roaring lion, looking for someone to devour." You must be on guard against him, just as Skippy should have been on guard for cats.

"The Bible also says that God knows about one sparrow falling,[2] so He knew about Skippy and must have permitted the bird's death for a reason."

Roger went to his room and thought for a while. He soon decided that his parents had a point. He told the Lord how he felt, pouring out his deepest feelings. When he had finished, the bitterness was gone.

He was glad the Lord hadn't let him go ahead and kill Kit-cat. Someday, when Jesus ruled, birds and cats would no doubt be friends, for the Bible said that the wolf and lamb would lie down together.[3] That was a time Roger looked forward to. In fact, he wondered if God had plans to have any birds in heaven.

---

[1]Romans 12:19
[2]Matthew 10:29
[3]Isaiah 11:6

# Punkin and Princess
## Make
## Peace

A FICTION STORY by Irene Aiken

"PLEASE, children," Mother said, as Sammy, 11, yelled at his sister who was only 9.

"Look! She ruined my poster board for school!" Sammy cried.

"But I didn't mean to," Amy said with her lip out. "It was lying here beside my coloring book and my paint water turned over."

"It's the only sheet of poster board I have!" Sammy continued. "Mother, why does she have to hang around when I'm doing my art work? Why can't she go play somewhere else?"

Amy gathered up her coloring book, her brushes, and paints, and moved away. She felt bad because it did seem as if she was always spilling something.

She stopped at the kitchen window just then and looked out. Their dog Punkin was chasing a cat. It looked like old Mrs. Wood's Siamese cat, Princess!

Amy ran to the door and opened it. The cat dashed right in and jumped into Amy's arms. Punkin followed at top speed.

Amy turned and ran with the cat, Punkin after them. "Help me, Mother!" Amy cried.

Mother shoved the kitchen stool at her and Amy climbed up. Punkin was a short-legged beagle. But he jumped and barked so loud the walls vibrated. Scared, the cat arched her back and dug her claws into Amy's helpful arms, then leaped to the top of the curtains behind Amy. Promptly the curtains, cat, and all came tumbling to the floor.

Punkin was usually a sweet-tempered animal who looked like Snoopy in the comics. He pounced on the cat all tangled in the curtains.

"Isn't that Mrs. Wood's cat, Princess?" Sammy asked.

"It doesn't matter whose cat it is—just get Punkin out!" Mother cried.

Sammy grabbed at Punkin and pulled him toward the door.

"It *is* her cat," Amy said. "And she never lets it out to run."

Just as Sammy opened the back door and shoved Punkin out, the cat untangled itself and shot out the door in front of the dog. Off the two animals went again, Punkin barking wildly as he chased Princess.

"Mother!" Amy cried, "Punkin will kill that cat!"

"He just might," Mother said, sounding desperate. She grabbed a leash and they all dashed out of the house, following the sound of Punkin's barking.

He was in the backyard of Mrs. Wood's house, when they found him—near her back porch. The cat was probably under there, but Punkin couldn't get through the narrow slats.

Sammy grabbed Punkin, and Mother got the leash on him. Then they started back home.

"I'm going to try to find Princess," Amy called after them.

"She went under the house, dummy!" Sammy yelled back at his sister.

"Come on, now, Sammy," Mother said, "we've got to get this dog home. And I don't like hearing you call your sister names."

"Well, she ruined my poster!" Sammy spouted.

"The Bible tells us to forgive one another," [1] Mother replied.

"Wait, Mother," Amy called after them.

Mother turned and looked back. "What is it?"

"I think Mrs. Wood is sick," Amy called. She was on the back porch, peering in a window. "She's sitting at the table, but her face is in her plate."

"Oh my! Sammy, you take the dog home and see that he stays there." Mother dashed back to Mrs. Wood's house and looked inside too.

"She's either ill or asleep," she said. "Let's try the doors." The back door wouldn't budge. Amy ran to the front. They couldn't open that either. "We'd better phone the police," Mother said, and they hurried home.

After phoning, they all walked back to Mrs. Wood's house and waited there till the police and ambulance arrived. Things happened fast then. The police got in. And the ambulance took Mrs. Wood away, its siren wailing eerily.

Amy left then and went home for her bank. She walked slowly down to the drugstore in town, taking her bank with her. She dug into it and bought a new piece of poster board for Sammy, then headed home.

Nobody had missed her. Too much had been going on.

---

[1]Ephesians 4:32

All the neighbors were still out in their yards, talking about how old Mrs. Wood must have had a stroke.

Amy liked Mrs. Wood, and felt sorry for her. She still wondered where Princess the cat had hidden. They hadn't been able to find her.

When Sammy saw the poster board, he was angry all over again. "You dummy! You got a yellow board. I need a white one."

"They were all out of white," Amy replied. "I'm sorry I messed up the one you were working on."

The next day, a man came to their door around suppertime. He had a cat carrier with him. "Does Amy Bender live here?" he asked.

"I'm Amy," she spoke up coming to the door behind Mother.

"My mother, Mrs. Wood, died this morning," he said. "We found a note in her jewelry box that said Princess should go to Amy Bender because she had run errands for her and loved the cat."

Stunned silence greeted his words. Then Punkin took over and began to bark loudly.

"We can't keep a cat here," Sammy said. "Punkin hates cats."

"We can teach Punkin to like her," Amy said, smiling. She was pleased that Mrs. Wood had remembered her.

"Nobody can make Punkin like cats!" Sammy said in his usual disgusted tone.

"If anyone can, Amy will do it," Mother said. She told the young man they were sorry about his mother and thanked him. He left the cat and went away.

"Here, set the cat carrier on the floor," Mother said. "Now, Punkin can get acquanted with her while she's in the cage."

Amy plopped down next to the two animals and talked

to them soothingly. "Nice doggie; nice kitty. You two have to become friends," she said again and again. Soon Punkin was whining instead of barking. Then he began to wag his tail at the cat.

Sammy watched, frowning. Then he shook his head in wonder, for Punkin had laid down next to the carrier and was grinning at Princess as if they'd always been friends.

"Amy," Sammy said then, feeling repentent. "I'm sorry. I've been really mean to you."

Amy shrugged. "You had a right to be mad at me; I did mess up your poster."

"I didn't have any more right to yell at you than Punkin had to bark at the cat. I'm sorry; really I am. You're not *stupid* at all."

Amy looked up. "Maybe brothers always yell at little sisters," she said, "the way dogs chase cats. But they can learn better if they try," she added, grinning. Sammy sat down on the floor beside Amy and stroked Punkin. "Could she be right, Punkin?" he asked the dog.

# Creature Features

by Gloria A. Truitt

An elephant has two big ears,
  A fish has none at all!
A spider is quite short compared
  To plaid giraffe who's tall!
There're humps on camels, wings on flies,
  And zebras wear fine stripes.
An octopus who lives down deep
  Has arms like curling pipes!
Now, if we think about God's plan
  For every living creature,
We'd know why He gives everyone
  A special, different feature!

63

# Animal Fun

FILCHOCK

"Oops! I'd better do something about this leak!"

"We shouldn't have taught him to bring in the paper. He always gets the comics first."

"He gets so dramatic when you tell him to play dead."

# The Champ

## A FICTION STORY by Darlene M. Eastman

THE small gray mare cleared the last jump with the ease and grace of a swan. The huge hall echoed with cheers and clapping. The girl riding the mare smiled warmly as she cantered from the ring.

Penny Wilson gritted her teeth and fought the tears. "Not again," she groaned. "Not again. I've worked Gazeame for months. Now Colleen takes her and wins."

Penny turned the bay gelding she was riding toward the horse barns. She hardly noticed the other riders anxiously waiting for their classes to be called to the arena.

She knew her mother would be waiting for her at the stalls reserved for the Saunders' horses. She also knew she would have to congratulate Colleen when she returned with her trophy and first-place ribbon. *It wouldn't hurt so much if I hadn't planned on showing that horse myself*, Penny thought.

Penny Wilson's father was the trainer and manager of Dr. Ed Saunders' well-known Arab-Angel Stables. Both Dr. Saunders and his 13-year-old daughter, Colleen, admired the Arabian breed and loved to show them to the public. Usually, they managed to ride in a few shows themselves and had Penny and her dad show them in many more.

But lately it seemed Colleen was riding in most of the shows herself. The problem was that Colleen always waited till the last minute to decide which horse she would show. And she always seemed to pick the horse Penny planned to ride. Since the horse belonged to Colleen's father, there wasn't much Penny could do.

Colleen had a terrible temper and in a short time had caused each horse to lose the split-second timing Penny's dad had worked so hard to get. Then she would go on to the next horse, leaving the one she'd spoiled for Penny's father to retrain.

Penny dismounted by the stable door. Noticing her mother walking toward her, she quickly turned her back and began to loosen the cinch.

"Penny, I know how you feel about Gaze-ame and how you've worked with her," her mother began. "But you know she belongs to Colleen. And—"

"Mother, please," Penny interrupted. "No lecture tonight. I can't—I can't understand why—" Then she began sobbing.

Martha Wilson put her arms around her daughter's shoulders. "Go ahead and cry," she said quietly.

"I'm sorry, Mother," Penny began, after the tears were dry. "If it were any horse but Gaze-ame, and any other class but jumping. It's just not fair."

"I know, Penny. But at least Gaze-ame proved she could jump. That's something to feel happy about, isn't it? No one thought a small Arabian horse like her could do it. I sometimes think your father even wondered, though I'm sure he wouldn't admit it now."

Penny was about to answer when Colleen rode Gaze-

ame over to where Penny and her mother were standing. She was in one of her better moods.

"Quite a horse I have, don't you think, Penny?" she asked. "And to think I never used to like her. We really showed them tonight, didn't we, Gaze-ame?" she said, dismounting. Just then she noticed some friends heading for the show ring and handed the reins to Penny, not waiting for an answer.

"See, Mother, she doesn't even care enough about a horse to loosen the cinch," Penny said bitterly as she watched Colleen walk away. "All she cares about is the attention she gets from the people who watch her ride."

"Sometimes God works in ways we don't understand," Mrs. Wilson said thoughtfully.

"But, Mother, how can a horse have anything to do with God?" Penny cried. "Especially in a situation like this?"

"I'm not sure, Penny. But God knows the answer," her mother answered quietly.

The next morning Penny helped her parents pack the saddles and other show equipment. They loaded the horses into the trailer and started the 350-mile trip home.

"I never thought this show would grow to such a big event," her father said as he turned onto the highway. "To think there were between 100 and 150 more entries this year. I was pleased that our horses did so well! Three first prizes, one second, three thirds. And then Gaze-ame taking that jumping class. Guess we did all right. I was worried when Colleen decided to ride the mare. She did OK though. You have to give her credit for that."

Penny flinched as her father mentioned Gaze-ame. As a Christian, she felt she shouldn't tear Colleen down in her father's eyes, yet she felt terribly wronged. Penny could feel her mother watching her, then the slight reassuring squeeze her mother gave her as she began to speak.

"Yes, Gaze-ame and Colleen did do a beautiful job. But, Fred, couldn't you speak to both Ed and Colleen?" she asked. "If they could let us know sooner which horses they plan to ride, Penny would be able to show the one that remained."

"I suppose I could," Mr. Wilson began. "Don't think it will do any good though. I think Colleen takes the one Penny plans to ride on purpose. I'll talk to them about it and see. I know how hard you worked with Gaze-ame, Penny. I'm sorry that it wasn't you who won the trophy. You certainly deserve all the credit for that horse becoming a great jumper. I wouldn't have taken the time to train such a small horse."

"Dad, I really wanted to ride her. But I'm glad she won. She's such a willing animal, and tries so hard to please her rider. I imagine Colleen will keep riding her now. Should I start riding Frasal, that little chestnut filly? Maybe I could have her ready for the Fort Denton show," Penny answered.

"We'll have to see, Penny. I'm afraid Frasal is too young and the Fort Denton show isn't that far away. Why don't you start working with her next spring? Be a lot better, I think. You'll still work with Gaze-ame, won't you? You know Colleen won't be riding enough to keep her in show shape."

"I suppose, Dad," Penny answered, "if that's what you want me to do. I'd like to ride at Fort Denton though."

"Why don't you try that dark gray mare Colleen rode last year, if you can get her jumping again. She's developed some bad habits."

Penny's heart jumped when her father said she should try Mai-tan. She was by far the most beautiful horse in the stables. Mai-tan was a fine-featured animal: beautiful head, straight legs, large intelligent eyes.

She was also the most independent horse Penny had known. She acted as if she were queen of the horse world and every creature should bow to her wishes. Mai-tan wasn't a mean animal—just strong-willed.

While watching Mai-tan glide through the pasture and leap over a small stream, Penny first dreamed of having an Arabian jumper. At that time Colleen was riding Mai-tan and Penny knew she couldn't use the horse.

But Colleen almost ruined Mai-tan that year. Many times she had taken the mare out to the arena and pushed her too far. Mai-tan would break into a canter and Colleen would jerk the bit and pull harshly on the horse's mouth. Then Colleen would lose her temper and the horse would become a bundle of nerves.

About the same time Dr. Saunders had purchased Gaze-ame. Gaze-ame was also a pretty horse, though not quite the beauty that Mai-tan was. Colleen paid no attention to the new mare, so Penny started training her. It wasn't long before Penny realized Gaze-ame had all the abilities of a jumper, plus a willing disposition.

Penny held Gaze-ame out of all the horse shows last year till she was sure the horse was ready. Dr. Saunders had watched her jump the mare many times and then Colleen became interested.

Just before the deadline for entering the classes for today's show, Colleen had entered the jumping class, riding Gaze-ame.

Colleen had finally given up showing Mai-tan and Mr. Wilson had turned the horse out to pasture, hoping that a little time might help the mare forget the harsh treatment she had received.

And now he had told Penny she could try Mai-tan!

The next day, Penny was up with the sun. She hurried out to the stables and brushed and curried Mai-tan. The mare seemed to know something different was going on as she nervously watched Penny's every move.

Penny talked gently to her till she calmed down and began munching her grain. After spending 20 minutes with the horse, Penny left to help with the rest of the daily feeding.

"Dad, please don't tell Dr. Saunders that I'm working with Mai-tan," she said, while helping her father train Gaze-ame an hour later.

"I don't plan to, Penny. No use getting him all excited till we see if you can do anything with her. It's too early to tell if she'll be any good or not. There's nothing the doctor would rather have than Mai-tan winning blue ribbons. She's always been his favorite."

"Thanks, I would rather Colleen didn't know either. I'm afraid she would ride her again if she knew I was training her," Penny said.

"What is it with you two girls?" Mr. Wilson stopped what he was doing and stared at Penny.

"I don't know," Penny answered. "Colleen just doesn't like me."

When Penny finished her chores, she saddled Mai-tan and rode to the arena. As soon as they entered the working area, Mai-tan became a bundle of nerves. She swished her tail, trotted sideways, danced around, and all but cantered in one spot. She soon was wet with sweat. Penny loosened the reins as much as she dared. Then she encouraged the horse to walk around the ring.

After several attempts, Mai-tan managed to walk almost all the way around the ring without dancing. Penny took the mare back to her stall and saddled Gaze-ame.

After easing Gaze-ame over each of the jumps, Penny

started back to the stables. Breakfast would be over if she didn't get to the kitchen soon.

The table was set and the smell of bacon filled the room as Penny entered.

"Good morning, Penny," her mother said. "How did it go this morning?"

"OK. I think Mai-tan will be ready for the Fort Denton show if she continues to do as well as she did this morning. She walked almost all the way around the arena. That's really something for her. She usually won't walk three steps without tossing her head and dancing around. Boy, would I like to get her in a show with Colleen and beat her."

"Penny! I'm surprised at you," her mother responded. "Do you think that's a good attitude to have? I hope this horse show business isn't going to change you."

"Don't you think the only reason you feel this way is that you want revenge on Colleen?" her father added.

"I don't know. You both always say to pray and keep your faith in God." Tears began forming in Penny's eyes. "But when someone hurts you and there's nothing you can do about it, what then? I've prayed and prayed, but bad things still happen. Colleen had no right to take Gaze-ame, even if it was her father's horse. I trained her!"

"Penny," her mother answered quietly, "try to understand as I tell you this—and don't get angry: Don't try to get even with Colleen—it will only bring you heartache."

Slowly Penny's anger melted. She realized that her prayers had been selfish. Penny had often asked God to help her get the things *she* wanted—not what *God* wanted. *Help me love Colleen—for Your sake, Lord,* Penny prayed silently.

"All right. I'll try to like Colleen. But it won't be easy and I can't guarantee the results."

Later that morning Penny was again out in the arena putting the horses through their practice jumps. She didn't resent working Gaze-ame even though she knew Colleen would be riding her in the Fort Denton show. At least she didn't resent it as much as she had earlier.

Penny was about to put the horse over the brush jump when she heard the voices of people entering the arena. She continued through the rest of the course before riding over to where her father, Dr. Saunders, and Colleen stood.

"Hi, everyone," Penny said, as friendly as she could make it sound. "Gaze-ame is certainly in good spirits this morning. Must be winning that championship last week, don't you think?" she said.

"Hello, Penny," Dr. Saunders answered. "She is a great horse."

"Do you want to take her around the course, Colleen?" Penny asked, dismounting. "She did so well for you at the show, I imagine you can hardly wait for Fort Denton."

"Why, yes," Colleen answered, sounding somewhat puzzled. She mounted and turned the mare to the jumping course. After completing the round of jumps, she returned to where the others were standing.

"That was good, Colleen," her father said. "I hope you and Gaze-ame keep getting along. What horse do you plan to have Penny ride at Fort Denton, Fred?"

Penny's father glanced at her, uncertain what to say, when Penny spoke up. "I'm going to work with Mai-tan, if it's all right with you, Dr. Saunders. Maybe she will be more settled this year than last. Anyway, I'd like to see how she works out for a few weeks."

Penny noticed Colleen's face redden. Penny hoped she hadn't done the wrong thing by revealing her plans for Mai-tan.

The two men walked away, discussing business matters. Colleen sat rigid on her horse till the men had left the building. Then she turned to Penny. "So now you plan to outshow me with Mai-tan, huh? You think just because she wouldn't work for me you can train her and outshow me. I'll have my dad sell her," she screamed as she started to turn away.

"Colleen, wait!" Penny shouted. "I don't want to outshow you. It's just that Mai-tan needs training and your dad thinks so much of her. Wouldn't it make you happy to see that mare bring home some ribbons for your dad?"

"You're not fooling me!" Colleen shouted. "You aren't at all interested in ribbons for my dad. All you want to do is show her before all my friends since she acted so bad for me last year."

Colleen jerked Gaze-ame around and galloped away. Penny ached inside when she saw the mare's puzzled expression at the mistreatment she was receiving.

Downhearted and disappointed, Penny returned to the house.

The weeks flew by and the Fort Denton show was drawing close. Penny continued working with Mai-tan and the horse was doing remarkably well. Penny decided she would only ride in classes that Colleen hadn't entered.

She was anxious for the evening to arrive so Dr. Saunders and her father could fill out the entry blanks and send them in.

Colleen had ridden Gaze-ame several times since she screamed at Penny. Every time she'd seen Penny work with Mai-tan, Colleen was cold and indifferent.

Penny had just finished saddling Gaze-ame and was ready to practice the jumps when she heard the stable door open and Colleen walked in.

"I'll work her myself," Colleen said, coldly. Then she added, "Why don't you saddle Mai-tan and come out? Gaze-ame seems to work better when there are more horses around."

Before Penny could reply, Colleen headed for the arena. Penny was puzzled but decided to go anyway. Besides, she wanted to work Mai-tan with more horses in the ring.

Colleen put Gaze-ame through her jumps beautifully. The successful jumps seemed to soften her feelings toward Penny, even to the point of thanking her for continuing to work Gaze-ame.

"Now let's see what Mai-tan will do," Colleen said sweetly. "She is such a beautiful horse."

Penny worked Mai-tan through her gaits, and the mare never missed a cue. Colleen smiled and watched each signal Penny gave as the horse eagerly responded.

Penny sang happily as she helped with feedings later that evening. Dr. Saunders and her father went into the stable office to fill out the entry forms for the big show.

An hour later, Penny and her mother were leaning on the white pasture fence, watching the colts at play. As her father walked toward them, Penny sensed something was wrong because he looked so serious.

"I—I don't know how to say this," he stammered. "But Colleen has entered both Gaze-ame and Mai-tan for herself. I'll look for a different job. It's just not right. It's just—" He couldn't finish speaking.

Hurt, anger, and bewilderment tore at Penny all at once. She couldn't believe it. Thoughts of God doing something for someone else, and all her mother's words bombarded her mind. *God? What God?* she wanted to scream. As hot tears rushed down her face, she raced to her bedroom.

Soon she heard her mother come into the room. Bitterly, Penny waited for her to speak.

"Penny, you—you are at a crossroads. Which way are you going to choose? You can quit riding and leave it to Colleen to do what she wants—or you can go on working with the horses and get them in top shape for the show."

"Work them for the show? Mother, you've got to be kidding!"

Didn't she understand what Colleen had just done? No mother could expect her daughter to go on turning the other cheek forever, especially when Colleen slapped it every time.

"Penny, I know this hurts you. God knows the suffering you're going through. Ask Him what you should do."

Puzzled and full of hurt, Penny knelt and prayed, *O Father, please take this bitterness from me. And show me how You want me to treat Colleen.*

"I think God wants me to go on working the horses, Mother," Penny said, after her prayer. "And He wants me to try not to hate Colleen."

Neither Colleen nor Dr. Saunders had been to the stables much since the day they sent in the entries. Dr. Saunders had taken the horses to the fairgrounds arena four or five times "to get them used to strange rings," he had said. Penny didn't have a chance to speak to Colleen before the Fort Denton show.

The show was bigger and better than ever. The weather was clear, and people came from all over to show their horses. Penny felt downhearted as she helped stable the horses and arrange the saddles and show equipment.

Show time was upon them and Penny watched breathlessly as Gaze-ame glided over her jumps with the ease of a deer. Colleen was a beautiful rider and, except for her vicious temper, she could become a top show-woman.

As soon as Penny finished watching Gaze-ame, she rushed to the barn. Two more classes and it was time for Mai-tan to enter the show ring for the first time in over a year. The mare seemed to sense Penny's tension. She stepped nervously around her stall. Penny's throat tightened as she thought of what Mai-tan might do once she was inside the ring. Penny was certain Colleen would blame Mai-tan's failure on her.

Stroking the mare, Penny talked softly to her. Reassured, the beautiful animal nudged Penny with her nose. Penny brushed and brushed the horse till her coat glistened.

Just as she led the horse from the stall, Colleen rode up, dismounted, and took Mai-tan's reins without saying a word.

"I'll be cheering for you," Penny called as they rode into the arena.

Tears formed in her eyes as Colleen and Mai-tan disappeared from sight. Penny brushed them aside and mounted Gaze-ame.

"I'll just sit on you by the gate. You won't mind will you, Gaze-ame?" Penny said as she turned the horse back to the arena.

The horses were just entering the ring when Penny rode up by the gate. She could hear them breathing as they floated around the ring.

Penny could tell the judge was impressed with Mai-tan. Her every move was beautiful. First the horses walked, then trotted, then cantered, then back to the trot.

On and on the show went as the judge called for the different gaits. All was going well till he called a halt. Penny's heart sank as she saw Mai-tan swish her tail, chew the bit, and begin moving nervously. Fortunately, the

judge was looking at another horse. Once again around the ring, and again—Halt!

Mai-tan was directly in front of Penny. As the mare began moving about, Penny could see Colleen's face redden with anger.

"Talk to her. Say anything. Just whisper," Penny called softly across the gate.

Colleen looked oddly at her then began softly reassuring the mare. Slowly she loosened the reins and relieved the pressure on the mare's mouth. Mai-tan didn't move a muscle.

The judge noted his paper and handed it to the speaker.

Penny screamed with joy when the judge called Maitan's name for first place. Colleen smiled broadly as she rode forward for the trophy and ribbon.

"Why, Penny? Why did you do it?" Colleen asked, after all the congratulations and the excitement were over. "After the way I've treated you, you helped me win that class. I just can't understand it." Tears began to stream down her face. "I hate myself. I'm so selfish, so miserable—so jealous of you," she stammered.

"Jealous of me!" Penny exclaimed. "How could you be? I don't have anything to be jealous of."

"Yes, you do! You work well with horses. You're always so nice. Everybody likes you. And you're happy!"

"It's because of Jesus Christ's love for me," Penny said softly. "You see, He has done so much for me. I—I can feel His love, Colleen. And you don't know how much I want to share it with you."

The two girls stood facing each other for a few seconds. Penny suddenly realized that her bitterness toward Colleen had been replaced by a strong feeling of love. Real love. God had answered her prayers.

She walked over and placed her hand on Colleen's shoulder. "Come on, let's go somewhere and talk."

# Porky,
## the Impatient
## Porcupine

A TRUE STORY by Joane G. Eby

JOANE HURRIED down the dry bush path. How hot it was here in Nigeria, West Africa! She looked toward the river. Only a few months ago it had been a raging flood. Now she couldn't even see the water. Nothing moved; even the waist-high grass stood still, for there was no breeze under the fierce sun. Everything waited for the cooling of late afternoon.

*It must be 120° today*, thought Joane. *Yesterday it was 110°, and today it's even hotter*. But to Joane it was a world of beauty. Growing up in Africa was exciting. She loved the Nigerian countryside. In the dry season it was dry and hot, and no clouds appeared in the light blue sky. In the wet season, rain clouds billowed overhead, and everything burst into lush greens and bright flowers that she loved so much.

She smiled when she thought of her grandmother in New Jersey. Grandma always seemed to feel sorry that Joane was missing all the nice American things. But Joane didn't feel sorry for herself. Africa was her home, and Africa was where she wanted to be.

"*Usi, abargu ra?* (Hello, how are you?)" asked an African as he passed by. He was returning from washing in the river. But already his forehead was covered with beads of sweat.

"*Usi, lapiya.* (Hello, I am fine.)" answered Joane. She liked the people and their interesting way of life. Many times, after spending all day in one of the markets, Joane would forget she wasn't one of the Nigerians. She would look at her hands in surprise. They seemed so pale, almost sickly, in contrast to the Nigerians' rich chocolate color. She laughed when she thought how funny she must look to them.

Joane also loved the animals. She had helped raise many kinds, from tiny field mice to good old Spunky-Spooky, the family's pet hyena. Right now she was on her way home to feed Porky, her pet porcupine.

As she walked along the path, she thought back to the time her father bought Porky from one of the Nigerians. The baby porcupine was so small she had to feed him every hour with an eyedropper. How tiring that was! At first she had to get up twice each night to feed him. There was no electricity in the house, and it was hard to handle a flashlight and Porky at the same time.

He was funny-looking then, as he didn't have any real quills; only a few long, thick white hairs. His legs were stubby, and he squealed like a pig. He was so small he fit into the palm of one hand.

Joane was glad she could feed him with a bottle now. His sharp little claws used to scratch her when she used the eyedropper. Now she only had to feed him during the day. He was eating the grass, bugs, and roots that were around him.

But Joane knew she would soon have to get him to drink milk from a bowl. She would be leaving home to go

to boarding school, and no one at home would want to give Porky a bottle every day.

Joane began to run down the path. Porky didn't like having his bottle late. He would angrily stamp his back feet, grind his teeth, and rustle his quills. She wondered how he would like drinking milk from a bowl. *It will probably make him very angry*, she thought. Porky always seemed to get upset at any change.

As she neared the house, her mother called to her from the window. "Joane, you'd better hurry. Porky is getting angrier all the time."

"Coming!" Joane called. She ran inside the house and grabbed the bottle of milk. Porky was running along the sides of his pen squealing.

Mada, the man who helped take care of all the pets, had already given Porky some grass and peanuts by the time Joane got there. Porky had dragged the grass all over the pen, and eaten most of the peanuts.

Joane settled down on the warm ground and began feeding him. He did like his bottle of milk! Each time he drank, he closed his eyes, stamped his back feet, swished his tail back and forth, and made soft gurgling noises.

Porky was one of Joane's favorite pets. Outside the pen he would follow her around like a dog. But he was getting harder to handle. He was more impatient, and he liked to raise his quills suddenly, when one least expected it.

He also wasn't very good when strangers were around. Joane remembered the day the school headmaster, Mallam Johanna, came to visit. As soon as Porky saw him, he raised his quills and raced backwards into Mallam Johanna. Fortunately, the headmaster was wearing a large flowing robe. Porky became so tangled up in the robe that he angrily ran off to another part of the house. It was then that Joane decided to keep Porky outside in a pen.

Joane sighed as she watched Porky gulp down the last few drops of milk. "Porky," she said, "you're going to have to learn to drink from a dish. Vacation is almost over, and no one will have time to give you this bottle when I'm away at school."

The next day Joane took Porky his milk in a large bowl. Porky ran to greet her at the fence. Joane entered the pen and placed the bowl on the ground.

Bewildered, Porky went over to investigate. He sniffed the bowl, then began to stamp his feet angrily. He rustled his quills and stepped into the dish, squealing and stamping frantically, splashing milk all over the ground.

Joane shook her head in disgust. "Well, maybe you'll drink it tonight if you don't get anymore this morning," she said. Porky wasn't listening. He was grinding his teeth and stamping around in the bowl of milk.

That evening Joane went once more to Porky's pen with a bowl of milk. Porky greeted her by frisking around the

pen. Joane noticed that the holes at the edge of the fence were getting deeper. He would be digging his way out soon. She placed the bowl on the ground. Porky snorted like a pig, shook his quills, and began to raise them.

"Porky!" scolded Joane. "Put those quills back down!" But Porky was busy pushing his nose under the milk dish. With a flip he had it upside down. Shaking his quills angrily, he stamped the last drop of milk into the dirt. After that he banged the bowl several times against the ground.

*Each time I bring him the bowl he gets angrier than the last time,* Joane thought. *What will he do tomorrow?*

The next morning when Joane went to Porky's pen he

was waiting at the dog house, making soft grunting sounds. He liked the warm patch of sunlight there. Joane put down the bowl of milk.

This time Porky had had enough. He rushed forward and bit Joane's wrist. Then he ran off to the far corner of the pen, raised his quills and began racing backwards at full speed.

With a startled cry, Joane jumped onto the top of the dog house to escape those dangerous quills. From the dog house roof, she watched Porky run around and around her, shaking his quills angrily and grinding his teeth.

*Oh, dear,* she thought, *I won't be able to get out through the gate fast enough.*

There was only one way out, and Joane took it. She leaped over the fence from the dog house roof, and headed for the house to clean up the bite Porky had given her. *I'd better put lots of peroxide on my wrist,* she thought. *It could get infected.*

"What happened?" asked her mother as Joane doctored the wound.

"Oh, that porcupine!" said Joane in disgust. "When it comes to milk, he'll never learn to drink from a dish. I'll just not give him any today. Maybe then he'll drink it tomorrow."

It was mid-morning by the time Joane was able to take Porky his milk. As she neared the pen, no Porky ran out to greet her. Mada came quickly. "I've been looking all over for him but can't find him," he said. "Do you see this big hole? He dug out of his pen during the night."

Just then Miriam, one of the village women, came carrying a large wooden box on her head. She did not look pleased.

"Is this your animal?" she asked as she placed the heavy box on the ground. "It was in our corn bin. My husband wanted to kill it and eat it. I thought it belonged to you, so I trapped it by putting some corn in the box. If it's not yours, I'll take it home and cook it. They are good to eat."

"Porky, Porky," Joane said, shaking her head. "You're becoming more trouble every day." Joane thanked the woman and gave her some corn to replace what Porky had eaten. By this time, Porky was panting heavily from being inside the hot box. He had had nothing to drink all morning.

Mada filled in the hole with rocks and Joane led Porky back into the pen. As she reached for the bowl of milk she stopped and looked at Porky. How big he had grown. His black and white quills were sharp as needles. They were at least 12 inches long, and some were as long as 18 inches. He was much too heavy for her to pick up. Father thought Porky must weigh close to 40 pounds. From the tip of his nose to the base of his tail he was 21 inches long.

"Milk, indeed!" said Joane. "Porky, you're a big porcupine. You are eating so many other things. Maybe you just don't want the milk. All you need is plain water. I'll give the milk to the cats." She filled another bowl with water and turned toward the house. As she left the pen, she looked back and grinned. Porky was rapidly lapping up the water. His back feet happily thumped up and down, and his tail swished back and forth.

"That solves one of the problems!" Joane exclaimed as she entered the house.

"Is there another one?" her father asked.

"I'm afraid so," she answered. "Last night Porky dug out of his pen. Now that he has done it once, he'll do it again and again. The older he gets the harder it will be to keep him in the pen. We can't take him out into the bush and let him go free. He's so used to being around people that he'd soon find his way to a Nigerian compound. After eating the people's corn and peanuts, it wouldn't be long before he'd end up in a pot of stew."

"That's one of the difficulties with raising wild animals as pets," her father said. "Sooner or later, it becomes a problem to keep them; but they can't be let go either. They often can't take care of themselves."

"Dad, do you think the zoo would take him?" Joane asked. "The zookeeper already wants Spunky-Spooky. Maybe he would take Porky."

"I can ask," replied her father, "but don't expect the zoo to take every animal you raise. There may already be a porcupine in the zoo, and they wouldn't want another one. Tomorrow I'll see what can be done."

The next evening Joane ran to meet her father as he neared the house. Her heart seemed to skip a beat. He was frowning. *The zoo must not want Porky,* she thought.

"They already have a porcupine," her father said before she had asked her question.

"What will I do now?" Joane asked in dismay.

"But—you're a lucky girl," continued her father. He smiled as he tugged at her blond hair. "The zookeeper says he'll take Porky. The porcupine they have is very old and won't live much longer. A new pen has just been built, and we can put Porky in it tomorrow."

Joane could hardly wait for the next day to see Porky's new home.

"Do you think he'll like it?" the zookeeper asked after Joane had led Porky into the new pen.

"I'm sure he will!" Joane exclaimed. "It's lovely!"

As Porky rushed off to a nearby bush, Joane looked around the pen. There were rocks, bushes, and trees. A small stream had been built along one side. The low wall around the pen had been made with cement. The zookeeper said the cement went several feet into the ground. That would keep Porky from digging out.

"Good-bye Porky," Joane called out. "As usual, he's not paying attention." She laughed. "Well, good-bye again."

This time Porky seemed to answer back with soft grunts. He had made his way to the stream and was rapidly lapping up the water, stamping his back feet and swishing his tail back and forth.

"Let's go, Dad," said Joane. "Porky's happy and so am I."

# God's Special Gifts

### by Gloria A. Truitt

Every living creature is
   Endowed with special things—
The kangaroos have pouches, and
   The condors, 10-foot wings!

Turtles poke along with shells,
   Gazelles run very fast,
And elephants can make a sound
   Just like a trumpet blast!

Now, if we'd look around the world
   At every creature known,
We'd see that God gives everyone
   A gift to call his own!

# All for a Duck

## A FICTION STORY by L. E. Eubanks

JEFF AUSTIN picked up the coiled rope lying on the porch and turned to his mother. "That poor duck I told you about is still on the log. It's soaked with oil from that tanker spill. I'm sure it can't fly. Maybe I can lasso it. If I don't get hold of it, it will starve."

"Bisquit has brought in a lot of ducks for you. Can't he get this one too?" his mother asked.

Jeff shook his head. "I'm afraid for him to try it in all that mud along the river. It's like quicksand. Even a little dog like Bisquit might sink. I'll get the duck some way."

Jeff headed for the mud flats along the river beside his home where he'd seen the mallard duck. The duck had evidently landed in the mud and oil. It must have struggled to the log and then was unable to fly because of the oil on its feathers.

It would die there if no one helped it, Jeff knew. He'd found other oil-soaked ducks, dead along the river. But he had saved some, cleaned them up and let them go.

Bisquit followed his master. "Good dog," Jeff said, ruffling the small spaniel's silky black fur. "If that duck

were farther out near open water, you could get it. You've saved a lot of them. This time you'll have to stay on the sidelines."

The duck was still on the log. Jeff was glad, for he had been afraid that it would try to swim. When he'd gotten as close as he could to the duck, it was still about 15 feet away with deep mud between them.

Jeff often practiced lassoing with a rope—the way he'd seen cowboys do at rodeos. He'd gotten pretty good. "I'll just try to get the loop over the duck's body then draw it tight," he told Bisquit. "Then I can pull him to safety."

He looped the rope carefully, then twirled it round and round. Just as he let it fly, the little cocker spaniel leaped out into the dangerous mud and headed for the duck.

"Bisquit!" Jeff cried.

He held his breath, watching helplessly. He would only increase the dog's danger by yelling or scolding him. Twice the spaniel almost went under. He looked nearly worn out when he reached the log, but he didn't stop to rest. He got hold of the oily duck and started back.

"Bisquit," Jeff moaned in silent agony. "You'll never make it."

The heavy slime was dragging the dog down. Without the duck, he might have reached Jeff. He was more than halfway back, when he gave up. Even then, he tried to hold the duck up as his own head went under.

Jeff looked down frantically at the rope in his hand. He couldn't use it now. The dog was too far under.

With a prayer in his heart, Jeff took a running leap. He landed in the mud next to the dog and immediately began to sink too. He got hold of Bisquit and pulled him up out of the sucking ooze. Thank God Bisquit was OK!

Jeff took the duck from the dog's mouth and tossed it to solid ground. It lay motionless, but Jeff had no time to think about it now. He was in danger himself.

"Lord, help me!" he gasped as he felt himself sinking fast. The heavy slime was above his knees. He could not pull his foot out to take a step. "I'm only about six feet from solid ground and I can't do a thing," he muttered.

He noticed the rope lying across the mud where he had dropped it. If only he could fasten it around that tree on the bank. But how could he get it around the tree? He groaned.

Bisquit whined and licked his chin. The dog seemed to know they were in danger. Jeff closed his eyes a moment. Then he had an idea. He reached for the rope and managed to get one end. He tied that tightly to Bisquit's collar. Then with Bisquit in one arm, he pulled the rest of the rope towards him with the other. He would have to toss Bisquit onto the river bank and hang onto the free end of the rope at the same time.

He wound the rope round and round his right hand.

Then with all his strength, he hurled his mud-caked dog through the air to solid ground. The small dog landed with a thud, but scrambled to his feet unhurt. "Stay!" Jeff cried, for Bisquit had started back into the mud. "Stay!"

Jeff was up to his hips now. He had to work fast. He looked around for something to throw. "Nothing like that out here," he muttered. "I *know*—my jackknife!" He jerked it from his pocket.

"Fetch it!" he ordered Bisquit as he hurled the knife out beyond the tree.

Bisquit ran to get it, but he returned on the same side of the tree. Jeff's heart sank. He had hoped Bisquit would run around the tree, taking the rope tied to his collar around with him.

Again the dog started out toward Jeff. "No, Bisquit!" Jeff cried again. "Stay!"

Nothing seemed to be working and Jeff continued to sink. His teeth chattered more from fear than cold. "Lord, now what?" Jeff gasped.

He searched his pockets. Only a small flashlight. He'd have to use his wrist watch too. "God, help me throw right and please make Bisquit go around the tree," he prayed.

"Bisquit," he called. "Drop it. Drop the knife!" The obedient little dog dropped the jackknife and stood expectantly watching his master. He seemed to know this was no ordinary game.

Jeff threw the small flashlight and Bisquit ran after it. Before he could turn back, Jeff called, "Fetch it, boy!" and threw his watch several feet on the other side of the tree. The spaniel reached the watch by running at a right angle from his first dash. He had carried the rope around the tree! "Good, boy! Bring it to me," Jeff called. Though he was sinking more slowly now, Jeff was up to his waist in the gripping mud. Breathing heavily, he held out his hands to the dog. Bravely, Bisquit again fought his way through the muck. Jeff pulled the tired animal out of the mud and took the rope from his collar.

Again, he tossed Bisquit through the air, praying that he'd land unhurt. And he did.

With both ends of the rope in his hands and the middle around the stout tree, Jeff pulled and fought his way back to solid earth. Safe at last, he lay for a long time, breathing heavily. Bisquit nosed around his face, whining.

At last Jeff sat up and hugged his dog. "Oh, Bisquit, I love you," he murmured. Then he laughed as he looked down at himself. "Mom will have a fit when she sees us!" he exclaimed.

Then Jeff remembered the duck. "Wonder if he's OK, Bisquit. Let's take a look." He walked over and picked up the duck. The bird struggled a bit in his hands as Jeff felt for broken bones.

Jeff grinned. "Looks as if we all made it," he told Bisquit, "thanks to a good God watching over us. C'mon let's take this bird and all go and get cleaned up."

# My Dog Valley

Told by Mark Houvenagle
Written by Shirley Houvenagle

I RACED out of school to see if the yellow and white collie was still leaning against the building. He had hung around the school grounds for almost a week. It was February and awfully cold out. I knew the dog was hungry. A couple of days before, I had brought him a sandwich and he had gobbled it down. Mom had said I could bring him home and feed him, but we couldn't keep him.

When I found the collie outside, he seemed weak. I called my friend Larry to help me. It was then that we discovered the dog had been hurt and couldn't walk very well. Larry helped me carry him home. I gave him some food, then let him out.

The next morning the collie was at school again but at recess he was gone. Some boys told me the dogcatcher had taken him away.

I asked Mom if she'd take me to the dog pound and she agreed. Sure enough, he was there. As soon as he saw me, he stood up in his cage and put his feet on the wire. He looked awfully sad and lonely.

The lady in charge said I could adopt him if no one claimed him within a week. Mom said I would have to pay

for him myself if I wanted him. I only had $6. The usual fee was $10. Every night that week I prayed that if it were the Lord's will, the dog would still be there when we went back.

A week later, on February 14, Mom drove me back to the pound. I rushed down the aisle through the cages of barking dogs, holding my breath. At last I found his cage and there he was! Then I went to the lady in charge to see if I could adopt him.

"How much money do you have?" she asked.

"Six dollars," I answered.

"Well, I think maybe we can give him to you for $5," she told me and wrote "special" on my ticket.

It sure was great, taking Valley home. I named him Valentine or Valley, for short (because that was the day I got him). He was the first dog of my own I ever had.

Before long I knew that Valley had not only been mistreated, he was sick too. Mom said we'd just pray that

God would make him well, and we'd take the best care of him we could.

It wasn't long before he was shaking my little brother's "popcorn" toy and growling with pretended fierceness. If I'd grab the toy, Valley would chase me and try to get it back. He seemed to feel much better. He became a great ball player too, even better than my older brother, because Valley never got mad.

A month later we moved to the country. Since Valley was crippled, we kept him in a dog pen when I wasn't playing with him. But one day in September, when I had gone to a friend's Mom let him out for exercise.

Some girls rode by on horseback. They called to him. Just then a car whizzed past and hit him. One of the girls came and got me. When I saw Valley, he was lying in the ditch by the road. He wagged his tail a little when I spoke to him.

Dad had just come home, so we took Valley to the vet. Once before Valley's back had been hurt. Now he was injured badly again, so the doctor put him to sleep.

I had thought Valley might die, but losing him was still hard to accept. We took his body home and Dad buried him during a rainstorm, way out in the pasture.

I went out the next day and cried beside Valley's grave, wishing that somewhere there was a dog heaven—and that I could see him again someday. Mom had said God promised eternal life only to people who accepted His Son as their Saviour. That didn't include dogs.

One of the Bible verses I had just learned before Valley was hit was Romans 8:28. It says, "And we know that all things work together for good to them that love God, to them who are the called according to His purpose."

I knew the verse applied to me because I had received Jesus as my Saviour when I was six. Then one summer at camp, I gave my life to God for His service. Still, when I thought about Valley and how much I loved him and missed him, I couldn't understand how anything good could come from his death.

The next day we went back to the animal shelter and just looked at dogs. All I could think about was that I'd never feel Valley's warm tongue on my hand again.

When we were leaving, a kind-looking man came over to our car and asked us what type of dog we wanted. He said his name was John Bode. He was a missionary, home from Southern Mexico. He and his family were now living in a place where no dogs were allowed. He had brought their dog to the shelter, hoping to find her a home.

His son Jimmy, who was nine, was sad because he didn't want to give Tippy away. She wasn't nearly as pretty as Valley but she was kind of cute.

We arranged with Mr. Bode for me to keep Tippy until his family could find a place where she could stay too.

Suddenly, because of Valley's death, I had a new pet and a new friend—Jimmy Bode.

Other good things came from Valley's death. Mom and Dad found out that the vet who put Valley to sleep had been sad and lonely since his wife's death. My folks went back to visit him—so *he* gained some new friends too.

Then we heard of a family who had so much sickness that they couldn't afford to keep their dog anymore. They said I could have Laddie if I'd take good care of him.

Laddie was a big, healthy collie who could jump as high as my head. Eventually he learned to play ball as Valley did. But he could never quite take Valley's place.

I still think about Valley at times. He'll always be special to me. I'm glad that I belong to Jesus Christ and have discovered He can make even sad things turn out for the best.

# Floss Finds a Friend

## A FICTION STORY by Elaine Brown

ANDREW longed for a kitten of his own—a fluffy white one. Then one day his mother came home from the shops, opened her basket, and said, "There you are; she's yours."

Andrew peeped in. "My own kitten!" He laughed with delight as he lifted out the soft white ball of fur. "I'm going to name you Floss 'cause you're as fluffy as cotton candy."

After tea, Andrew wrapped his warm scarf around Floss and took her for a walk in his arms. He felt proud when people said, "What a beautiful kitten!"

"Jesus, thank You for Floss," Andrew said, giving her a hug. "You must be very clever to make such a lovely kitten!"

At the end of the road, Andrew stopped to look through the broken fence outside the last house. Old Miss Pringle lived there and Andrew felt sad whenever he passed by. The cracked windowpanes and the peeling paint on her door all seemed a part of her lonely life.

101

"Watch out for old Mrs. P. She doesn't like little boys—or cats," an older boy shouted to him.

Andrew shivered. He unzipped his jacket, hid Floss inside, and hurried home.

The days became warmer. Everything was growing, even Floss. She liked to sun herself on the doorstep, waiting for Andrew to run in from school. When he picked her up, she would purr and rub her whiskers against his cheek. "You're my best friend," Andrew told her.

But one afternoon Floss wasn't there. *Maybe she's inside,* Andrew thought, opening the door. "Floss, I'm home!" he called.

But there was no sign of his half-grown cat. "Floss!" he shouted again, hoping to hear the patter of paws across the floor.

"I think Floss has gone for a walk," his mother said. "She'll be back for supper."

Andrew frowned and went out to look for Floss. She *always* waited for him. Something must have happened to her.

At bedtime Floss was still missing. Andrew looked sadly at her basket then went to his room, trying to keep back the tears.

"I'm sure Jesus is looking after her," Andrew's mother said gently. "And He knows where she is even though we don't."

"Dear Jesus, please keep Floss safe," Andrew prayed. "And please tell her to come home again soon."

The next morning Andrew had an idea. "I'll ask everyone I meet if they've seen Floss," he told his parents at breakfast.

But no one had seen the white cat, not even the policeman or Mr. Bright, who whistled while he cleaned windows. "Do you ever clean Miss Pringle's windows?" Andrew asked.

"No, but I whistle when I pass her gate, just to cheer her up," Mr. Bright said, smiling.

Summer came and went. Golden leaves danced down from the trees and chased Andrew as he walked home from school. He wondered if Floss was enjoying her first fall.

Just as he passed Miss Pringle's, the front door opened and the old lady stepped out. Andrew felt scared, remembering all he'd heard about her. Suddenly, he saw a flash of white. It began at her door and ended at his feet. The flash was Floss!

For a moment Andrew's bounding heart stood still. Then with a cry of delight, he picked up the cat and cuddled her. How heavy she'd grown. "Floss, you're bigger and better than ever!" Andrew said, laughing.

He didn't notice Miss Pringle walking toward him till she asked, "Your cat?"

"Yes!" Andrew spun around angrily and looked straight into the old lady's face. He had another surprise. Her face was kind, and her many wrinkles seemed to turn into a hundred smiles. Andrew hung his head.

"I've been looking after her for you," the old lady said. "She's such a gentle cat and—." When she stopped, Andrew looked up and saw a tear running slowly down her face. "—She's been a real friend."

Andrew looked at Floss. It felt so good to hold her again. "I'm going to take her home now," he said. And without looking back, he ran off, holding Floss tightly.

Once again, Floss welcomed Andrew home from school. She purred like a motor when he picked her up. But now she often sat on his windowsill all morning, watching the street.

He began to wonder if she was thinking about the old lady. He remembered the tear on Miss Pringle's face when he took Floss away. "But she's mine!" he told himself, and felt happy again.

One afternoon Floss and Andrew were sitting by the window. He stroked her long soft fur and put his face up against hers. She nudged him and purred loudly. He laughed. Then he remembered Miss Pringle's face—the wrinkles turned into smiles. *It was Floss who made her smile too, but now she'll be feeling sad again.*

For a moment Andrew sat quite still. He was struggling, deep down inside. "Jesus, please help me do it," he whispered. Then he stood up, lifted Floss into his arms, and hurried from the house.

The sun had set and a cold wind blew. Andrew wrapped his scarf around Floss as he ran down the street. When he reached Miss Pringle's house, he walked slowly up to the old front door, then knocked.

It was a while before the door opened. "I want you to have Floss," he told the old lady. "So you'll feel happy again."

Miss Pringle's wrinkles creased into a puzzled frown. "But—" she began.

"She's yours," Andrew said quickly. He gave Floss a last hug, then put her into the old lady's arms and ran all the way home.

When Christmas vacation came, Andrew visited Miss Pringle every day. He'd sit on a thick rug by her fire while Floss purred beside him.

"Are you sure you want me to have Floss?" Miss Pringle asked him one day.

"Oh, yes," he said.

Miss Pringle smiled. "Now I have two friends."

Early one morning Andrew woke up to strange splut-

tering sounds on his window. "It's snowing!" he yelled,
flinging back his covers.

The pure white flakes reminded him of Floss, so he
hurried out along the quiet street to visit her.

Miss Pringle opened the door before he knocked. "It's a
very good morning." She winked at him as she let him in.
"Full of surprises."

Andrew was puzzled. Then he saw Floss on the rug—
and two balls of fluff lying beside her.

"Floss!" Andrew cried, kneeling beside her. "You have
a family!" He stroked her and her kittens gently. Floss
purred and strutted around proudly.

Andrew and Miss Pringle both laughed. "Well,

Andrew, which one do you want?" Miss Pringle asked.

Andrew looked up. "A kitten—for me?" He watched them a moment. "Well, when she's ready to leave Floss, I'd like the ginger-brown one. I'll call her Toffee!"

He picked up Toffee, oh so carefully, and held her just a moment before giving her back to her mother. "Floss, you sure have made me happy!" he said.

"Me too," Miss Pringle added.

# A Nuisance in Ma's Kitchen

**A FICTION STORY by Arleta Richardson**

WHEN GRANDMA called from the backyard, I knew I was in for it. It was her would-you-look-at-this voice, and that usually meant I was responsible for something.

I ran out to where she was hanging up clothes. "What, Grandma?" I asked.

"Would you look at this?" Grandma said. "I just went into the kitchen for more clothespins, and came back out to find this."

"This" was one of my kittens. It had crawled into the clothes basket and now lay sound asleep on a clean sheet.

"If you're going to have the kittens around the house, you'll have to keep an eye on them. Otherwise, leave them in the barn where they belong. It's hard enough to wash sheets once without having to do them over again."

Grandma headed for the house with the sheet, and I took the kitten back to the barn. I didn't agree that it *belonged* there. I would much rather have had the whole family of kittens in the house with me. Later I mentioned this to Grandma.

"I know," she said. "I felt the same way when I was

your age. If it had been left up to me, I would have moved every animal on the place into the house every time it rained or snowed."

"Didn't your folks let any pets in the house?" I asked.

"Most of our animals weren't pets," Grandma said. "But there were a few times when they were allowed in. If an animal needed special care, it stayed in the kitchen. I really enjoyed those times, especially if it was one I could help with."

"Tell me about one," I said.

"I remember one cold spring," Grandma said. "Pa came in from the barn in the morning carrying a tiny goat. Ma hurried to find an old blanket and a box for a bed.

" 'I'm not sure we can save this one,' Pa said. 'The nanny had twins last night, and she'll only let one come near her. I'm afraid this one's almost gone.'

"Ma had opened the oven door and put the box on it. Now she gently took the little goat out and laid it on the blanket. It didn't move at all. It just lay there barely breathing.

" 'Oh, Ma,' I said, 'do you think it will live? Shouldn't we give it something to eat?'

" 'It's too weak to eat right now,' Ma said. 'Let it rest and get warm, then we'll try to feed it.'

"Fortunately it was Saturday," Grandma continued, "and I didn't have to go to school. I sat on the floor next to the oven and watched the goat. Sometimes it seemed as though it had stopped breathing, and I would call Ma to look.

" 'It's still alive,' she said. 'It just isn't strong enough to move yet. You sit there and watch it if you want to, but don't call me again unless it opens it's eyes.'

"When Pa and the boys came in for dinner, Reuben stopped and looked down at the tiny animal.

" 'Doesn't look like much, does it?' he said.

"I burst into tears.

" 'It *does* look like much!' I howled. 'It looks just fine! Ma says it's going to open its eyes. Don't you say things to discourage it!'

"Reuben backed off in surprise, and Pa came over to comfort me.

" 'Now Reuben wasn't trying to discourage that goat,' he said. 'He just meant that it doesn't . . . look like a whole lot,' he finished lamely.

"I started to cry again, and Ma came to the rescue this time.

" 'Crying isn't going to help that goat one bit,' she said. 'When it gets stronger, it will want something to eat. I'll put some milk on the stove to heat while we have dinner.'

"I couldn't leave my post long enough to go to the table, so Ma gave me my plate to hold in my lap. I ate dinner with an eye on the goat, and I was rewarded by seeing it move and open its mouth.

" 'It's moving, Ma!' I said. 'You'd better bring the milk!'

"Ma soaked a rag in the milk, and I held it while the little goat sucked the rag greedily. By the time it had fallen asleep again, I was convinced that it would be just fine.

"And it was," Grandma continued. "By evening it was standing on its wobbly legs and baa-ing loudly for more to eat.

" 'Pa, maybe you'd better bring its box into my room,' I announced at bedtime.

" 'Whatever for?' Pa asked. 'It will keep warm right here by the stove. We'll look after it during the night. Don't worry.'

" 'And we aren't bringing your bed out here,' Ma said, anticipating my next suggestion. 'You'll have enough to do to watch that goat during the day.'

"Of course Ma was right. As the goat got stronger, he began to look for things to do. At first he was contented just to grab anything within reach and pull it. Dish towels, apron strings, and tablecloth corners all fascinated him. I was kept busy trying to put things out of his way.

"From the beginning, the little goat took a special liking to Ma. She was not flattered.

" 'I can't move six inches in this kitchen without stumbling over that animal,' she spluttered. 'He can be sound asleep in his box one minute and sitting on my feet the next. I don't know how much longer I can tolerate him in my kitchen.'

"As it turned out, it was not much longer. The final straw came one Monday as Ma prepared to do the washing.

"Pa had placed the washtub on two chairs near the

woodpile. Ma always soaked the clothes in cold water first, then transferred them to the boiler on the stove. I was in my room when I heard her shouting.

" 'Now you put that down!' she said. 'Come back here!'

"I ran to the kitchen door and watched in fascination as the goat, with one of Pa's shirts in his mouth, circled the table. Ma was right behind him, but he managed to stay a few feet ahead of her.

" 'Step on the shirt, Ma,' I shouted, 'then he'll have to stop!'

"I began to run around the table the other way, hoping to head him off. The goat seemed to realize that he was outnumbered, for suddenly he turned and ran toward the chairs that held the washtub.

" 'Oh, no!' Ma cried. 'Not that way!'

"But it was too late. Tub, water, and clothes splashed to the floor, and the goat danced stiff-legged through the soggy mess with a very surprised look on his face.

" 'That's enough,' Ma said. 'I've had all I need of that goat. Take him out and tie him in the yard, Mabel. Then bring me the mop, please.'

"I knew better than to bring the subject up to Ma, but I was worried about what would happen to the goat. If he couldn't come back in the kitchen, where would he sleep?

"Pa had the answer to that. 'He'll go to the barn tonight,' he said.

" 'But, Pa,' I protested, 'he's too little to sleep in the barn. Besides, he'll think we don't like him anymore!'

" 'He'll think right,' Ma said. 'He's a menace, and he's not staying in my kitchen another day.'

" 'Well, I like him,' I said. 'I feel sorry for him out there alone. If he has to sleep in the barn, I'll go out and sleep with him!'

"The boys looked at me in amazement. 'You!' Roy said.

'You won't even walk past the barn after dark, let alone go in!'

"That was true," Grandma said. "I had never been very brave about going outside after dark. But this time, I was more concerned about that little goat than I was about myself.

" 'I don't care,' I said stubbornly. 'He'll be scared out there, and he's littler than I am.'

"Ma didn't say anything, probably because she thought I'd change my mind before dark. I didn't, though, and when Pa started for the barn that evening, I was ready to leave with him. Ma saw that I was determined to go, so she brought me a blanket.

" 'You'd better wrap up in this,' she said. 'The hay is warm, but it's pretty scratchy.'

"I took the blanket and followed Pa and the goat to the barn. The more I thought about the long dark night, the less it seemed like a good idea, but I wasn't going to give in, nor even admit that I was frightened.

"Pa found a good place for me to put my blanket. 'This is nice and soft,' he said, 'and out of the draft. You'll be fine here.'

"I rolled up in the blanket and hugged the goat to me as I watched Pa check the animals. The light from the lantern cast long shadows through the barn, and I considered asking Pa if he wouldn't like to stay there with me. I knew better though; and too soon, he was ready to leave.

" 'Good night, Mabel,' he said. 'Sleep well.' And he went out and closed the barn door behind him. At that moment I doubted whether I would sleep at all. If it hadn't been for the goat and the certain knowledge that the boys would laugh at me, I would have returned to the house at once.

"I closed my eyes tightly and began to pray. In a few

moments the barn door opened again, and Reuben's voice called to me. 'Mabel,' he said, 'it's just me.'

"He came over to where I lay, and I saw that he had a blanket with him.

" 'I thought I'd sleep out here tonight too,' he said. 'I haven't slept in the barn for a long time. You don't mind do you?'

" 'Oh, no,' I said, 'that's fine.'

"And I turned over and fell asleep at once.

"When I awoke in the morning, the goat and Reuben were both gone. I found the goat curled up asleep beside his mother.

" 'Will you be sleeping in the barn again tonight?' Ma asked me at breakfast.

" 'No, I don't think so,' I said. 'I'll take care of the goat during the day, but I guess his mother can watch him at night.' "

Grandma laughed at the memory.

"After I grew up," she said, "I told Reuben how grateful I was that he came out to stay with me. I wonder how my family ever put up with all my foolishness."

Grandma went back into the house, and I wandered out to the barn to visit the kittens. I decided that I wouldn't be brave enough to spend the night there—even with a big brother to keep me company!

# Buttons

## A TRUE STORY by Jeanne Hill

"YOU'RE SURELY not going to keep that good-for-nothing stray," my Uncle Buck said to Daddy as the two men walked past me into the house.

I was sitting on the porch steps, holding our newly-found dog, Buttons. Angry tears slid down my cheeks into her fur. I'd have thought my big, bespectacled uncle was heartless if I hadn't seen the tears and respect in his eyes the day his favorite hound died. Trouble was, he just didn't know Buttons!

Just the week before, during the first snowstorm of 1939, the wind had carried a haunting whine. That cry had led our family—my dad, mother, Josie, 13, and me, 10,—across our snow-covered Ozark farm near Rolla, Missouri to a briar patch.

There we found a tiny, wispy-haired dog, caught fast on sharp thistles. Daddy picked her up and carried her home. We cleaned and combed her and named her Buttons because she had black, buttonlike eyes.

All the family fell in love with Buttons—except Uncle Buck, my daddy's brother who owned a nearby farm.

Uncle Buck just couldn't understand why Daddy would keep a dog he couldn't hunt and track with.

Right there on the porch steps, with a chilly wind whipping around me and Buttons, I said a secret prayer. I asked God to help Uncle Buck see just how worthwhile Buttons was.

Though we went to church and often had prayer in our home, that was my first real, from-the-heart prayer.

I never dreamed the Lord would give me such quick assurance. My uncle had only just gone when Mama called us to supper. As usual, Daddy took out our worn Bible.

Now, I'd heard him read several verses from that Bible at suppertime every night of my life. But the verses had never spoken right to me before. He was reading from Zephaniah 3. When he got to the last part of verse 19, my heart started skipping rope.

" 'I will save her that halteth, and gather her that was driven out; and I will get them praise and fame . . . where they have been put to shame,' " Daddy read.

*Buttons* had been driven out. God was telling me that my prayer would be answered, I was sure. Uncle Buck, who had "put her to shame," would someday know what a great animal she really was!

I went to sleep that night, still thinking about my private message from my Lord. Yes, God had changed in my thinking from *the* Lord to *my* Lord. And I was glad for the change.

But weeks and months went by without another sign from heaven. Buttons kept a watchful eye on the mother hens, strolling with their young. She didn't rest till the hens and chicks were safely closed into the brooder house at dusk.

Once, in the meadow full of bluebells, she sent a hawk

flapping frantically for his life. He had swooped down to catch a young chicken.

Unfortunately my uncle was never around to see such feats. And the promise I'd heard from the Bible faded somewhat from my mind as the weeks passed.

All that summer, Buttons stayed close to Josie and me. She scouted out the blackberry patch before we picked the purple fruit. She rolled in the fresh dirt when we hoed the garden.

She ran ahead of the one of us who milked the cow. She chased rabbits in the ravine where Josie hiked. And she lay on the cool ground beside me under the fox grapes in the glen.

On warm honeysuckle evenings, if I read, Buttons lay on my lap. And if I was catching lightning bugs, she trotted beside me.

On a hot August afternoon, Uncle Buck came over. He was going to leave at choretime to feed his hogs, but Mama spoke up. "Let your boys do that this evening, along with the milking. You stay for supper."

An offer like that was too good for a widower to pass up. So Daddy and he continued to talk while Mama lit the lamp and started peeling potatoes. Josie beat me to the milk pails, so I took the egg basket from its hook, and we went outside together.

The yellowish twilight was giving way to night. Dusk piled up in fence corners. It shrouded trees and hung suspended in the air like an intangible curtain that made it hard to see. But we knew the paths well.

I gathered the eggs and filled the nests with fresh straw. Then, basket brimming, I took the shortest path to the kitchen with my heavy load of eggs.

As I neared the cistern, I saw Josie coming from the barn with Buttons. A moment later, on the path beside the brooder house, my world went wild.

I remember smiling to myself when I heard the mother hens in the brooder warn their baby chicks sharply as my bare feet padded past their house. But I soon realized it was not my presence that had prompted their warning!

As my right foot came down beside the brooder, I sensed movement in the grass along the path. But my left foot had already come up and was on its way down again. I stepped on something slick! It slithered beneath my heel!

"Snake!" I screamed, jerking up my foot. "Snake!" At my erratic footwork, the heavy egg basket lurched to one side. Eggs flew into the air and spattered all around me, and I fell hard on my back. Breath knocked out of me, a cold terror moved into its place. I felt the snake slithering along my side!

I heard Button's growl as I stared, horrified at the yellowish tan snake. It was so close now, I could see it was a deadly copperhead!

The next instant I felt the stiffened ridge of fur along my dog's back as she jumped against my side. Snapping at the snake, she was able to seize it for only a moment. But she flung it a few feet away from me—feet that bought me safety!

Then, before the copperhead could coil, Buttons jumped between the snake and me, trying for a good hold. The snake, however, shifted and got away from her.

I scrambled to my feet as Mama came running with a lamp and held it high. Josie followed with Daddy. Uncle Buck trailed with his shotgun.

Uncle Buck raised his gun. But the swift struggle between dog and snake made it impossible for him to get a shot at the snake. Only Buttons' skill could save her now.

I held my breath as I watched the snake coil and the dog jump away and try to get a death grip. Finally the flurry of

fur and snake quieted and Buttons stood there with the snake's neck clamped tightly in her jaws.

She shook the snake violently till all the life was gone. Then she dropped it and came to me. I picked up the exhausted little dog, and she lay panting in my arms while I shook from the effects of fear.

Mama and Daddy took us inside to check us carefully for bites. "Nothing on you," Mama reassured me when she finished checking me. "How about Buttons?"

Uncle Buck's specs were far down on his nose as he examined every inch of fur. "Not a mark," he said at last. "Ya know, that copperhead was well nigh bigger than that dog." He came over and tousled my hair. "Yes sir! That dog of yours is mighty fine after all!"

That's when I remembered my Lord's promise. For, standing there staring at Buttons, Uncle Buck had that same look of respect in his eyes that I'd seen the day his prized old hound had died.

Other books in the
ANIMAL TAILS SERIES

## The Hairy Brown Angel and Other Animal Tails

*Grace Fox Anderson*
Our bestselling collection of 22 true and true-to-life animal stories that make excellent devotional reading. (6-2475)

## The Peanut Butter Hamster and Other Animal Tails

*Grace Fox Anderson*
More amusing stories that picture God's love for all His creatures. (6-2484)

## The Incompetent Cat and Other Animal Tails

*Grace Fox Anderson*
These 32 short stories, poems, and cartoons will delight readers with fascinating facts and animal fun. (6-2495)

## The Duck Who Had Goosebumps and Other Animal Tails

*Grace Fox Anderson*
From such animals as a chipmunk, a lamb, a cow, a pony, a goose, and a duck, you will learn lessons about making friends, setting a good example, and accepting people the way they are. (6-2476)